I0731618

FIENDS AND FAMILIARS

DEBRA DUNBAR

CHAPTER 1

TYPHON

"*L*ord." The demon bowed low before me, which was quite a feat since his nine-foot, half-fish/half-owl form wasn't optimal for the motion.

"What?" I'll admit my reply was a little snappy, but I was busy torturing a mass murderer and I hated to be interrupted.

"I heard from Bifrons, who says he got the news from Quitta, who supposedly found out from Nubar—"

"Get on with it, fiend. I've got a busy schedule today and this soul isn't going to torture himself." I looked over at the human, wondering if that were true. Some of them were very adept at delivering the sort of self-punishment even we demons would shy away from.

"We may have found *him*."

I immediately forgot about the human, knowing exactly who "him" was. I'd forbidden my demons from mentioning Faust's name for the last two hundred and forty years, ever since he'd gone missing and not even my most skilled hellhound had been able to find him.

The guy had signed a contract with a crossroads demon,

then somehow managed to keep himself alive for three hundred years—in spite of all sorts of attempts on our part to kill him. Finally, he died and his soul was delivered unto our hands as per the contract. He wasn't here a week before he disappeared. Gone. Poof.

And worst of all, I'd been the demon assigned to supervise his punishment. A soul escaped hell while on my watch. It was mortifying. The only reason Satan hadn't demoted me was because it was clear that Faust had help.

It was those poor suckers who felt Satan's wrath. And while I was glad it wasn't me, Faust's escape was a blot on my otherwise perfect record. I needed to get him back. And I'd been trying to find the sneaky bastard for two hundred and forty years.

I was thrilled at the thought that we may have finally found him.

"Where is he?"

The fiend, and Satan knows I couldn't remember any of their names, took a hasty step backward at my tone.

"It might not be *him*. I'm getting this information fifth hand, and it could be faulty," he warned, raising his hands as if to ward off my expected anger.

I wasn't angry, I was excited. "Tell me."

He gave me an address then wiggled an outstretched hand. "That could be off by a few houses, or even a few miles though. The demon who says he sensed *him* isn't all that good at location or directions. And *he* supposedly is ambulatory. That's what I heard, anyway."

Ambulatory? As in he was moving about by his own free will and had somehow evaded all detection for hundreds of years? Or perhaps he was trapped and the bastard who had him was changing his location occasionally to help avoid detection?

Either way, I'd find him. Glancing over at the human and

remembering my schedule, I reconsidered my initial impulse to drop the burning hot whip and race to the mortal plane. It wouldn't be the first time rumors had been wrong, and I didn't want to appear an idiot, or seem as if I took my infernal duties less than seriously. No, I'd send one of my hellhounds to check out the validity of this fiend's claim. And if it proved to be true? Then I'd rearrange my schedule a bit and give myself enough free time to take care of a matter that had caused me no end of worry and anger for the last two hundred years.

CHAPTER 2

ADRIENNE

"There's another one!" The woman screamed, clutching her ample bosom as I raced after the scampering squirrel.

Normally my pest control and wildlife removal company was the easiest job ever thanks to my magical talents. Waltz in. Tell a colony of a few hundred ants to go elsewhere, relocate a huge wasp nest from someone's eaves to a remote tree, convince a dozen bats to take up residence in the comfy bat boxes I'd constructed rather than an attic. I spoke to animals, and they generally were amenable to doing my bidding.

Not these squirrels. They were determined to stay in this woman's house. Basically, they'd given me the middle finger, and told me if I wanted them to move, I'd need to catch them. Which is why I'd been here for an hour, chasing the furry things all over. I'd caught three, but this last one was proving to be a clever little bugger.

Drake hissed and hopped from foot-to-foot, causing the woman to shriek once more. She wasn't all that happy about my co-worker, but Drake had been my constant companion for the last three weeks. I think he was what the spell books would have called a familiar, but I hadn't done any rituals to bring one to my side. He'd just sort of appeared one day and never left.

Most witches who had familiars seemed to get a cat. Figures that I'd get a turkey vulture with a six-foot wingspan and a bright red, bald head. I don't know what had possessed me to name him after a hip-hop artist when he looked more like Lurch from the *Addam's Family*, but the name had stuck, and he would be forever known as Drake.

"Could use a bit of help here," I complained to the vulture. He cocked his head at me and I realized I probably didn't want his help. Turkey vultures didn't have the sharp talons that birds of prey had. His chicken-looking feet were better suited for holding down long dead carrion than snatching a running mouse from midair. His beak could do some serious damage, though. That thing was like a scalpel. I'd seen him pick a pig's head clean down to shiny bone in less than an hour. One stab and that squirrel would be shish kebab.

I might be a bit annoyed, but I didn't want the furry little guy dead. I just wanted him in the cage with his brothers.

The squirrel darted out from behind the fridge and the woman screamed again, swinging wildly with her broom and by some incredible luck actually hitting the animal. It went airborne and I dove, catching it before the thing took a header into the cabinetry.

Don't bite me, I told it, hoping the fact that I'd saved the squirrel from a minor concussion might work in my favor. Normally animals happily did whatever I asked. Not today.

The squirrel bit me. I let out a curse, but kept a tight hold on the thing, wishing I'd let Drake skewer it after all.

Shoving the squirrel in the cage with the others, I turned to accept a check from my client. She also handed me a paper towel to soak up the blood that was covering my fingers and threatening to drip onto her carpet.

"Let me know if you have any further pest or wildlife problems." I smiled through my pain and recited the usual blah, blah, blah that would hopefully get me either repeat business or a referral.

She nodded enthusiastically. "I will. You're the only one who's been able to catch them. I called three others and none of them could. They even put out traps and poison, but the squirrels wouldn't go near any of it."

I was thankful for that—well at least about the poison. I didn't mind humane traps, but ones that injured or killed the animal weren't something I'd ever use or approve of. And I hated poison. Of all the terrible ways to kill something, that was the worst in my opinion. I'd seen what poison could do to a mouse and I wouldn't wish that death on a cockroach.

Actually, I kinda liked cockroaches. Of our family of witches, only Babylon's specialty was considered weirder than mine. That plus the fact that we were the youngest of seven sisters made us rather close. A necromancer and a witch who could communicate and persuade animals to do her bidding. We were an odd pair, but then again all my sisters were odd—even the ones with more conventional witchy skills.

I left my client with a handful of business cards and loaded the cage of squirrels in the back of my truck. Drake hopped along beside me, jumping into the passenger seat and promptly rolling down the window. There was a fall nip in the air, but the bird liked to feel the wind in his feathers, so I left the window open and turned the heat on as I pulled down the driveway.

This had been my last job of the day, and I was looking forward to a relaxing evening at home. All I had to do was drop these squirrels off somewhere far enough from my client's house that they wouldn't be back, then I could enjoy a hot shower, some leftover takeout ribs and a glass of wine.

"What do you want to watch tonight?" I asked Drake as I maneuvered the truck onto the highway and toward the mountains.

The vulture made a hissing noise, but thanks to my magical ability, I perfectly understood him.

"I'm not watching the *Angry Birds* movie," I told him. "Pick something else."

He tapped his beak on the dash.

Rio.

I sighed. "How about something that's not a cartoon? We saw *Up* last night. Let's go for a romance, or drama or something not animated."

I'd enjoyed *Up*, although I'd seen it a dozen times before. Drake had been particularly fond of the scenes with Kevin the bird in them—go figure—and I never failed to cry at the part where Carl's wife, Ellie, dies.

Was that a spoiler? I hope it wasn't a spoiler.

Drake hissed again.

"*The Birds* is a classic," I admitted, "but I'm not sure I'm in the mood for horror tonight. How about we watch *Ladyhawke*, and save *The Birds* for tomorrow night? I'll even scrape a possum off the side of the highway for you to eat while we watch. Put it on a plate for you and everything."

Drake seemed to think this was a good compromise. I turned on the radio as we took an exit and headed up the mountain toward the pass that marked the boundaries of Accident. I figured that would be a good place to turn loose a group of belligerent squirrels. There was plenty to eat, lots of good spots to stay warm during the coming winter, and the werewolves would most likely ignore them since they preferred to hunt larger prey.

I pulled down an unmarked dirt road, throwing the truck into four-wheel-drive as we bounced over potholes and some tree limbs that had fallen during the last storm. About a mile in I put the truck in park and got out. Drake joined me, but took to the air as soon as I lowered the tailgate. The squirrels were not happy. I tried to tell them how wonderful this place was, and how peaceful it was going to be here without some woman screaming at them all the time, but they weren't having any of it. It seems they'd grown fond of indoor living, and were not interested in making their home out here in the wilderness.

Finally I gave up trying to convince them and just unlocked the cage. When none of them budged, I grabbed the handle and upended the thing, trying to dump them out on the ground. They held on for dear life and I resorted to shaking the cage and trying to pry their little paws off the wires. One fell out and promptly jumped into the cab of my truck. Another bit the tip of my finger, making me drop the cage onto the ground.

"Ooo! So sorry about that!" I squeezed my finger, blotting the blood on my shirt as I bent to make sure none of the squirrels were hurt. That's when they made a break for it.

I shrieked as one used my head as a launchpad, then fell back onto my ass, scrambling out of the way and shielding my face with my hands. Thankfully none of the squirrels attacked me.

Not thankfully, none of the squirrels ran into the woods either.

So there I was, sitting in the dirt with another bite on my hand, watching as the last squirrel jumped into the cab of my truck after the others. That's when Drake returned and dropped a very dead, very bloated, very rotted weasel at my feet.

At least he hadn't dropped it on my head.

"Lovely. Is that your dinner, Drake? Possum not your choice for tonight? Maybe you can put it in the truck bed then help me get these squirrels out."

He grabbed the weasel carcass and tossed it into the bed of the truck. I picked up the cage and motioned for him to stand guard at the driver's-side door and make sure any squirrels I ejected didn't get back inside.

Then I went in.

The next half hour was like a Keystone Cops film. Those squirrels were agile bastards, leaping all over my truck as I tried in vain to grab them. Sweaty and frustrated with my hair half out of its ponytail, I gave up. It wasn't going to be easy driving home with a bunch of squirrels in my truck, but I didn't seem to have any alternative to that besides spending the night here in the woods. That *wasn't* an option. I wanted my hot shower. I wanted my leftover ribs. And I wanted to sleep in my own bed tonight.

Drake climbed into the passenger seat, and I got in. The car started and I saw a furry head poke out from under the seat. Drake hissed, and the squirrel vanished with a squeak.

"That's your job, buddy," I told the vulture. "Make sure none of them mess with me while I'm driving. None of us wants me to wreck tonight."

Drake agreed with a guttural sound, then got to work glaring and hissing at any squirrel he saw as I drove. By the time I pulled into my driveway I'd realized my mistake. I should have been the one standing guard while Drake went in to herd the squirrels out of my truck. They actually seemed to be listening to him, which they certainly weren't doing to me.

The motion-sensor light came on and I saw a large, dark shape standing in front of my porch, looking particularly eerie with the lighting behind it. Drake danced from foot to foot on the passenger seat, communicating his unease. Was it a lost dog? Stray animals did seem to find their way to my house, sensing that I'd take care of them and find them a good home— and make room for them in my home until that happened. The thing did seem vaguely dog shaped. Newfoundland? Although it didn't seem quite that furry from its outline. Mastiff?

It followed us. Drake told me.

Followed us from where? The squirrel lady's house? The woods? From down the street? The latter had to have been what Drake meant, because I hadn't seen any dogs chasing after my truck as I drove down the highway.

I got out of the car, dismayed to see the squirrels race out before I could close the door. They took one look at the big dog and shrieked. Drake got out of the truck so fast he nearly knocked me over. Then he half ran, half flew around back to pop the tailgate open, grab his dead weasel, and take to the air.

Jerk. He'd never run from a dog before, but this did seem to be a particularly huge dog. At least he'd removed the dead stinky thing from the back of my truck. Hopefully he'd eat it before he returned and I wouldn't have to deal with that smell in my house.

I left the tailgate open to air out the truck, grabbed a handful of treats that I kept in one of the crates, and walked slowly and non-threateningly toward the animal. It stared at me, its eyes seeming to glow orange with the reflection of the light.

"Hey boy. It's okay. You're safe here."

The dog held still as if it wasn't even alive. I reached out with my magic and instead of the easy flow of communication, I got nothing. Was it even an animal?

"Babylon?" I called out, wondering if my sister was playing a trick on me. It wouldn't be the first time she'd surprised me with some zombie animal.

I took another two steps toward the...thing. "Babylon? Come on, Lonnie. This isn't funny. Send your dead dog back home and we can have a glass of wine. I've got leftover ribs."

My sister didn't appear. The dog still remained completely still. I was beginning to sweat a little. Okay, more than a little.

Two more steps and I was finally in a position to better see the dog. It was the size of a mastiff with black wiry hair and a strange musculature. The way its front legs bowed out, it made me think the animal could possibly stand on its hind legs, or that it had a greater range of motion than most canines did. Since my magic wasn't having any affect, I fell back on plan B and tossed a few of the treats toward the creature. Hopefully he liked freeze-dried liver.

The dog-thing lowered its head to sniff at the treats, then his lips curled back revealing huge sharp teeth. A long forked tongue snaked out and slurped up the bits of liver.

Okay. Well at least I knew it was alive and liked treats. I contemplated whether it would be a better idea to keep trying to make friends with this thing and at the very least ease past it to get into my house unmolested, or if I should give up and go around to the back door. The thought that this thing might come after me the moment my back was turned made up my mind. If I was going to have to fight off a toothy animal, I was going to do it head-on.

"Good doggy. Good boy. Can I get inside? I'll give you some leftover rib bones later if you let me in."

I tossed a few more treats, trying to lure the dog-thing off my porch and away from my door. He slurped them up, following the trail, but as I took another step forward, his orange eyes lasered back on me.

"Easy boy. I won't hurt you. Why are you here? Do you need help? A place to stay?"

I didn't know if it was the liver treats or if my magic was somehow getting through to the creature, because he cocked his head, a puzzled expression on his face. Random thoughts and emotions washed over my mind, as if they were making their way to me through a thick blanket.

It was a fierce beast, trained to seek, find, and kill. It was confused about why I could see it and how I was managing to communicate with it. And it really liked the liver treats.

"I've got more in the truck," I told the dog-thing. "And I know you'll like the rib bones as well. Why don't you let me get you some water and more to eat?"

I tossed the rest of the liver treats into the grass next to the porch, and while the creature ate them, I casually walked up the steps to my door as if this was absolutely an ordinary occurrence to find a strange dog beast on my porch.

The noises the thing was making as it ate the liver treats were setting the hairs at the nape of my neck on end, but I kept my breathing steady and unlocked my door. As soon as I pushed it open, I felt the creature's attention snap to me once more.

There. I sense it. Master was right.

I stood in the open doorway and faced the creature, not sure if I should slam the door shut and bolt it or not. It curled its lips back again, and I swear its teeth grew longer. The thing hunched down as if it were about to spring and I sucked in a breath, my hand gripping the door.

A hissing noise and the flapping of giant wings rent the silence. Drake descended from the sky, landing on the porch between me and the dog-thing. I froze, unable to retreat inside and leave my vulture friend to fight this thing himself.

I shouldn't have worried. Drake extended his wings outward, opened his beak, and hissed. I don't know if it was the sight of the huge bird, the threat of the knife-sharp beak, or the stench of long dead weasel on his breath, but something made the dog-thing take a step backward. He snarled at Drake, then snarled at me.

"Get back," I told Drake as I prepared to do something I hated—something I'd sworn I'd never do.

Drake hopped aside, and I locked eyes with the dog-thing, but before I could unleash my spell, he vanished.

"Stupid preternatural dog-thing," I muttered as I scanned my yard to see if he'd just teleported across the street or something. Thankfully none of my neighbors seemed to have been disturbed by my standoff, because out here in the world away from Accident, supernatural beings and magic were supposed to be the stuff of fantasy. Not that I hadn't been able to explain away all sorts of odd things in the month since I'd bought this house. It was amazing what people believed when the alternative was even more unbelievable.

Deciding that I'd rather relax and eat ribs than go searching for the dog-thing, I went inside. My house wasn't particularly big. In fact, it was fairly indistinguishable from the other cookie-cutter one-story homes in this neighborhood, but I liked it. It had been a difficult decision to move out of Accident, where my kind of weird was less weird, to out here in the "real" world, where I couldn't hang with shifters, fae, vampires, and goblins at the local bars. Practicality won out, though. The majority of my clients were outside of Accident and it was a much shorter commute if I lived here.

The real bummer of living here was how isolating the last month had felt. I hadn't any friends outside of Accident, so I'd thrown myself into my work and was beginning to feel a bit depressed at my lack of a social life. I *should* go over to the bar where my youngest sister worked and maybe meet some people, but those darned squirrels had worn me out. Ribs, pajamas, and *Ladyhawke* it was. Tomorrow was Sunday and family dinner night. That would give me some much-needed interaction with non-feathered, two-legged beings.

True to my word, I threw the rib bones out into the yard

in case the dog-thing came back and set a bowl of clean water out for him. The whole time I was eating I kept hearing a scurrying noise in the attic. By the time I started streaming the movie, the scurrying noise was in my kitchen.

Well, I *had* been complaining about how lonely I was. I didn't expect the universe to send me four squirrels, though. I looked over at Drake and he shrugged. That's when a furry little head peeked around the corner of my sofa at me.

They *were* pretty darned cute, even if they refused to listen to me and had taken up residence in my house without even saying please. Three other heads looked around the sofa and I stared back at them. I had a choice—I could spend the evening chasing these guys down, putting them in a cage and shoving them into the garage, or I could give up and resign myself to the fact that I might have some roommates throughout the winter—in addition to Drake, that is. Just as I'd been too tired to go hunt down the dog-thing, I was too tired to repeat my earlier Keystone Cops performance of running around after squirrels, so I popped an extra bag of popcorn, set a few bowls on the floor, then grabbed the larger bowl for Drake and myself on the couch. It didn't take my new roommates long to come out of hiding and dig into the popcorn. Once they realized I wasn't going to snatch them up and stick them in a crate, they relaxed and actually sat down to watch the movie with us.

They were all four gray squirrels, but it was clear that the larger one was the leader of the bunch. The others looked to him frequently, following his lead. He was a little over twenty inches long and looked to be close to two pounds in weight. His bushy tail held more white than the others, and his ears had little black tufts of fur on them. Every now and then he shot me a wary glance, but I didn't blame him given that we'd all gotten off to a rocky start.

Once the movie was over, I hit pause and addressed my

new roommates. "Okay guys, here's the deal. You can stay and I'll provide an assortment of nuts and other food for you, but you can't go trashing my house or getting into the garbage."

They all chattered in excitement, once again looking toward the big guy for guidance. He turned to me and asked where they were to sleep.

Heck if I knew. There was a spare bedroom, but I liked to keep that available in case one of my friends or family from Accident came to visit and decided to stay the night.

"How about the attic?" I asked, knowing that's where squirrels tended to make their home. "I can put some old towels up there for you all to nest in."

The others seemed on board with that, but Big Guy shook his head. It seemed the idea of sleeping in the attic made him nervous. He wanted to sleep in my bedroom.

Great. Drake had already claimed the footboard of my bed as his. I'd tried to kick him out but gave up when I awoke every morning to see the giant vulture perched there. But four squirrels and a vulture?

What the heck. It's not like I had a sex life to speak of. "Okay, but no running around in the middle of the night. I need to get my sleep, and if you all wake me up, you're out of the bedroom. Got it?"

Big Guy nodded.

"So…what do I call you?"

The other three squirrels tilted their heads. I wasn't surprised. Animals often didn't understand our need to give them names. They seemed to communicate just fine without them, and in all honesty I could speak to them so they knew which one I was talking to. But I liked names. It showed that I respected these animals. And they *were* my roommates, after all.

"Oak, Maple, and Pine." I pointed to each of the squirrels in turn.

Big Guy held up his little paws and chattered, saying he already had a name but that it could not be spoken.

Huh. Poor guy to be saddled with some unpronounceable name. "So what should I call you? Sequoia?" He was the biggest, after all.

He flicked his tail and squeaked indignantly, but didn't offer up any further suggestions. Drake hissed that I should call him Pain-In-The-Ass. That seemed a bit long, so instead I decided to call him Hemorrhoid—Rhoid for short.

The squirrel seemed pretty pissed off about that, but too bad. If he wasn't going to offer up an alternative and didn't like Sequoia, then Rhoid it was. It did seem to fit him. And if he'd spent his whole life with an unpronounceable name, then this couldn't be much worse.

Per Drake's request we followed up *Ladyhawke* by watching *The Birds*—not exactly the best choice right before bedtime, but I hated to disappoint the vulture. The squirrels were quite alarmed by the plot and twenty minutes in, Oak, Maple, and Pine were all hidden behind me on the couch. Every time the birds would attack, the three made loud *kuk-kuk* noises as they would to warn each other of predators in the wild. Rhoid proved to be more stoic, sitting by the empty popcorn bowls while the movie played—although at one point he did edge a little closer to me.

When the credits had finished rolling, I turned off the TV and went around the house doing my usual check. Stove was off. Doors were locked. Wards were in place. I glanced outside and saw that the rib bones were gone. Either the dog-thing had come back to get them or some other neighborhood canine had discovered the treat. I didn't sense anything particularly odd, so I finished my nighttime routine and went to bed.

A huge monster came to me in the night, chasing me through the woods. He had long white fangs, glowing red eyes, and horns, and I could not persuade him to stop. Suddenly I was at my truck, and trying to trap the monster in a cage, but each time I thought I had him, he'd break free. I tried to get in the truck to drive away, but the doors were all locked, so I ran.

My legs moved like they were stuck in molasses. He was closing in on me, his breath hot against the back of my legs. When he tackled me I braced, expecting my body to hit hard against the ground. Instead I bounced on something soft and cool, and opened my eyes to see that I was on a bed.

The monster rolled me over, pinning me on the mattress with his body. I should have been terrified, but I wasn't. Heat shot through me and I arched against him, wanting this creature like I'd never wanted anyone before in my life. His red eyes raked down my naked body and I writhed, breathless and desperate to feel him inside me. He rocked his hips and I gasped as he slid across my wet folds. Now. Oh now. Why was he waiting? Why were those damned squirrels making so much noise?

Squirrels. My eyes flew open and I scrambled to get out of bed. The sheet tangled around my legs and down I went onto the floor. Rhoid's dark eyes stared at me from under the bed, his little paws clasped tightly together. Oak, Maple, and Pine were sounding their alarm, and Drake was joining in with a series of hisses and beak-clacking. I managed to get myself untangled from my bedsheet and ran to the window, calling my magic to me. I was very limited in what I could do, but an intruder would definitely be deterred by ants swarming all over him, or owls dive bombing him.

There on the front lawn was the dog-thing. He was sniffing around the lawn, but as I looked at him, his head swiveled and his eyes met mine.

They glowed an orange-red. But unlike the monster in my dream, I didn't feel either scared or turned on. No, I felt annoyed. This guy had interrupted a really good dream—a dream in which I was about to get laid, a dream in which I'd been about to have some mind-blowing, epic sex. I hadn't had the real thing in quite a while, and a dream like that was as good as it was going to get, even if I had been about to have sex with some horned, fanged monster.

I yanked open the window and leaned out, not caring if I woke the neighbors or not.

"Hey! Yeah, you. Asshole. I fed you liver treats. I fed you rib bones. Now get lost. Go on."

The dog-thing stared at me in amazement. I felt his confusion, felt him wishing there were more rib bones on the lawn. Then he vanished just as he'd done before.

I slammed the window back down, still pissed off that my dream had been interrupted. Would it continue if I went back to sleep? Probably not. With my luck I'd have a dream about rolling in sticker bushes, or finding one of Drake's roadkill dinners in my fridge. Glancing at the clock I realized it was three in the morning—far too early for me to get up, especially on my day off. Climbing back into bed, I bundled the sheets and blankets up around me. That's when I realized something.

I was naked. Why was I naked? I'd been wearing pajamas when I went to bed.

Sitting up, I flicked on the light. My pajamas were crumpled and across the room on the floor. Chuckling, I got up and put them back on.

"That must have really been an amazing dream if I stripped down while asleep," I said to myself.

Getting back into bed and turning off the light, I lay there for a while, trying to go to sleep. I'd been kind of nasty to that dog-thing. True, he'd woken me out of a really good dream, but it's not like he'd known that. It hadn't been his fault. And I *had* kind of encouraged him to come back by feeding him and putting the bones out for him. Sighing, I rolled over and resolved to be nice to the dog-thing if he returned. If he was here in the morning, I'd give him breakfast. Maybe I'd even invite him to stay. Might as well. I had a vulture and four squirrels in my house. One big dog-thing wouldn't make much of a difference.

CHAPTER 3

TYPHON

*Y*eth stood before me on his rear legs, a long line of drool hanging from his jowls.

"Master, I went to the address you gave me and picked up the scent. He was there. He definitely was there."

"Was?" Had I lost him again after searching for so long?

"I searched the area and found nothing but a human woman. I traced his scent and discovered that he'd left in a conveyance, so I began to search the city, using the distinctive odor of the conveyance. It smelled of dead things, of creatures, of human and greasy take-out food."

I nodded, waiting for Yeth to continue. That bastard Faust wouldn't escape me this time.

"There was a dwelling...it smelled strongly of the conveyance, but not of the soul you seek, but as I was checking the house, the conveyance arrived—and I smelled him. I sensed him. He's there. He's hiding, but I felt the brush of his essence. He's there."

"Is this my torture?" The soul next to me moaned. "To

stand here while you both yammer on about vehicles smelling of greasy take-out food?"

The damned, they were so impatient. Turning away from Yeth, I unscrewed the cap from a bottle of milk and sniffed it. Ugh. It was so horribly spoiled that there were chunks floating in it. Perfect.

"Well, why is my lost soul not *here*?" I asked Yeth. "You sensed him. Why did you not bring him to me?"

Yeth eyed the milk, sniffed it, then made a gagging noise. "I…I wasn't able to retrieve him, Master. He is there, though. I am positive he is there."

I handed the milk jug to the human soul I was torturing. "Drink this, then get on the treadmill." He knew better than to argue. The soul chugged down the chunky milk as quickly as he could then shuddered. "Hurry it up. No dawdling. Get on that treadmill." The soul groaned, but did as I said. I turned the machine on, then cranked it up all the way. Once the soul started retching as he ran, I turned back to Yeth.

"Then go back and get him. What's the delay? I've waited for centuries. I don't want to wait any longer."

"Ummm." Yeth dropped down onto four legs. "There was a woman."

I frowned. "So? Remain invisible to the human eye, and go bring me my lost soul."

Yeth stared at the ground. "That woman…I don't think she's a regular human."

The soul on the treadmill made a heaving noise. "Don't you puke. You puke and it's another quart of spoiled milk." I pointed a finger at Yeth. "What in the third circle are you talking about? What woman? And what do you mean she's not a regular human?"

"The one who owns the house where *he* is. I don't think she's totally human. And she's got a really big pet bird. I mean seriously big. It's got a sharp beak and it hissed at me."

I rolled my eyes. Yeth was terrified of birds. This pet was probably a parakeet and he'd peed himself at the first chirp. "Do I need to send in another hellhound?"

Yeth stood up on his hind legs, holding his front paws up in front of him. "No! No, Master. I can…I can face down the bird. I'll go back."

I had my doubts about Yeth, but I was a fair demon and I believed in second chances. Sometimes.

The hellhound left and I turned my attention back to the politician on the treadmill. He was a writhing puking mess on the ground and I'd moved on to torturing one of those guys who ran the Nigerian prince scams when Yeth returned.

"He's definitely in the house, Master," the hellhound announced.

I spread my hands wide. "Did you not hear me before? Bring him to me."

Yeth squirmed. "The human woman has something around her house that prevents me from entering. Although she was kind enough to throw me some very tasty rib bones. They weren't as good as the liver treats she gave me earlier, but I quite enjoyed them."

I couldn't believe this. Yeth used to be a decent hellhound, fear of birds aside. What had happened to him? Why was he suddenly turning into a lap dog over liver treats and rib bones?

"Go back and bring him to me. I don't care if she gives you a T-bone steak, get in that house and bring him back. Understand?"

"But Master, there is something around the house that—"

I waved my hand, inadvertently smacking the scammer in the head with the whip I'd been holding. Oh well. He deserved it.

"I. Don't. Care. Go. And don't come back without him."

Yeth took off with his tail between his legs, and I renewed my efforts to punish the scammer.

"It's impossible to get good help," I complained to the man. "Maybe I should send Barghest instead. Or Cerberus."

The man moaned.

"I know, I know. Still, I shouldn't *have* to go myself to do such a thing."

I really shouldn't, but perhaps I was trusting Yeth a bit more than I should. With his fear of birds and his apparent weakness of being bribed by meat products, I worried he might fail once more.

"Here." I handed the whip to the scammer. "Keep hitting yourself with this. I've got something I need to do."

Heading out into the mists, I made my way past the torture rings and into the residential areas of hell. I didn't often use my home because work was so incredibly enjoyable. Why would I want to do something such as sleep or socialize when I lived for my job? There was no need for hobbies when my nine-to-five was my hobby. When you love what you do, then it's not really work, is it?

But for this I needed to concentrate, and that was hard to do with souls screaming and wailing.

My residence was a bit stark and smelled of brimstone—which was understandable since it had probably been two months since I'd been there. I brushed the ashes off my bed and sprawled across the crimson sheets, resting my horned head on the pillow. Just a quick peek, and then I'd get back to that scammer. I'd just project myself into the mortal plane, using Yeth's location for guidance. Once he had Faust's soul, then I'd return to my work. But if the hellhound got distracted by liver treats or scary giant parakeets, then he was going to find himself the one drinking a quart of spoiled milk and running on the treadmill.

I closed my eyes and projected myself, racing through the

ether, across the fields and to a completely unremarkable neighborhood. If I hadn't seen Yeth skulking his way across the lawn, I would never have known this was the house. They all looked exactly the same. What a perfect place for Faust to hide. With a blink my spirit was inside the house, inside a bedroom that did not smell like brimstone and did not have ashes on the sheets. I took a second to orient myself, and noticed the truly giant bird on the footboard of the bed.

Huh. I guess Yeth wasn't exaggerating after all. That really *was* one big-ass bird. I waited a second to see if the vulture could see me, but he remained asleep. Reassured, I opened up my senses and took it all in. There was a lingering scent of buttery popcorn coming from outside the bedroom, and a stronger aroma of vanilla and ginger inside. The bedroom was a bit of a mess with clothes tossed in piles, and wrinkled clean laundry in a basket. A dresser sat off to the side with cosmetics, a few books, and a bra on top. I couldn't help but pick up the bra, because hey, I might be a demon, but I'm a guy. And I'm nosy.

It wasn't a very exciting bra. Nothing lacy or red or silky. It looked like the kind of underwear human females wore when jogging or going to their gyms. I heard something stir, and quickly put the bra back.

The noise came from the bed. I glided over, hoping to find Faust under the covers with the woman who owned the utilitarian bra, but there was only one occupant in the bed— the woman. I caught my breath, thinking I had been very, very wrong in my assumptions about this woman from her choice in bras. But before I could do more than admire her silky auburn hair, I was sucked unwillingly into a dreamland.

By Satan's leathery wings I hated this. Human dreams blew. You never knew what you were going to end up doing. I could wind up salsa dancing with an elephant, or I could find myself discussing embroidery with a blue-haired woman who smelled like medical ointment. But this time I found myself chasing the woman through the woods.

Oh, hell yeah. Now *this* was a good dream. She was wearing a gauzy white thing that did nothing to hide the sweet curves of her ass as she ran. Her auburn hair swung around her shoulders, her bare feet pounding through the leaves on the dirt trail. Just as I was closing in on the woman, the dream changed. Suddenly we were beside a truck. The woman faced me, and I'll admit I was suddenly struck speechless.

I'd thought she was beautiful as she slept, but here, awake in a dream, she was gorgeous. She was fucking jaw-dropping sexy in that gauzy thing that was suddenly so short it barely covered her crotch. Not that it mattered. I could see her long muscular legs, her round breasts, the curve of her hips and the slim line of her waist as if she were standing naked right before me. Her mouth opened, and I found myself transfixed by her lips.

Then she screamed and began throwing cages at me—cages that opened and encased me, trapping me in a mesh of wires. I'll admit, it only turned me on further. For her, a human, to face down a horned, glowing-eyed demon and try to cage him? That took some serious balls. Or the female equivalent.

I melted the metal of the cages, only to have her continue to throw them at me. Just as I was beginning to think I was going to spend the whole night breaking out of cages, this sexy woman moved away, the dream changed again and I found myself once more chasing her down.

But this time it was different. It was almost as if she wanted me to catch her. The white gauze vanished and she was naked, her pace about half of what it had been before. I easily caught up to her, inhaling the smell of the vanilla and ginger lotion on her skin as I wrapped my arms around her and took her to the ground.

Only we weren't on the ground. We were in her bed, and her warm brown eyes stared into mine, filled with desire. It was as if she wove a spell around me, as if I were trapped far more securely than those wire cages could ever have done. By all that was unholy, I wanted this woman. I rubbed against her, everything but my need for her fading from my mind. Then just as I was about to seal the deal, an infernal sound filled my ears. Some horrible *kuk-kuk* noise. The woman vanished from under me and I fell—fell through the ether and back to the ashy sheets of my own room. The smell of popcorn and lotion was replaced by that of brimstone. I sat bolt upright in my bed, now knowing why Yeth had been so afraid of that bird, why he'd been seduced by the liver treats and rib bones.

Seduced. *I'd* been seduced as well, and not by scraps of food. Me, Master of the Hellhounds.

I'd been seduced by a witch.

CHAPTER 4

"Adrienne, does the vulture really need to be inside?" Cassie asked, glaring at Drake. "We made Hadur's raccoon stay outside."

"And I think that's a horrible way to treat a member of the family," I countered. "Diebin is just as important as Lucien."

The demon bristled at my comparing his value to that of a raccoon and a vulture, but I ignored him. He might be the son of Satan, but I knew he enjoyed our family squabbles. Did he have any brothers or sisters, I wondered? Maybe we could have some giant multi-family holiday dinner. We'd need to rent a conference hall because I didn't think there was room enough in our family home for even the Perkins' extended family.

"Drake isn't going to eat the meatloaf or get up on the table," I told Cassie. "He brought his own meal."

The vulture's meal was outside. Even though I insisted Drake be allowed to socialize with the rest of us—because vultures were extremely social creatures—I did agree that the groundhog roadkill he'd picked up off the side of the highway needed to be as far away from our own dinner as possible.

I looked around at what had always seemed like an enormous dining room and winced. Honestly if our family got any bigger, some of *us* might need to eat outside just from a lack of space. We were seven sisters, and our cousin Aaron, all over for Sunday dinners, but five of my sisters had shacked up which meant instead of eight, we needed to set a table for thirteen. Our table didn't hold thirteen, so Cassie had added a folding card table to the end along with those metal folding chairs typically used at funerals. We all drew straws each week because no one wanted to sit at what amounted to the kids' table.

Lucky for him as well as us, Aaron was off on a weeklong cruise he'd been suckered into by some time-share spiel the travel agent had given him. That meant we could all squash along the dining table, cheek-to-jowl, rather than four of us drawing the short straw for the kids' table.

I'm not sure which was worse, being teased for ending up eating on the card table, or packed so tightly against my family that I could barely raise a fork to my mouth. I looked around, thinking that if Cassie knocked out a wall, or stuck an addition onto the back of the house, we might be able to get one of those enormous U-shaped conference tables and use it for dining instead.

This Sunday I was here early, feeling the need for family time—for human interaction. Cassie hadn't even started the meatloaf yet. The two of us were peeling potatoes while Lucien sat at the kitchen table and snapped fresh green beans. It was kinda funny that the son of Satan was prepping veggies for dinner, but I kept my amusement over that to myself.

"So how's your week been?" Cassie asked as she waved a potato peeler.

"Not bad. There's lots of bat removal now that the babies are out of their nests and I can legally evict them. I include two bat boxes with every service, and even hang them up for people. It's important to educate folks on the value of having bats in their neighborhood."

Cassie didn't look particularly interested in hearing about that, so I didn't elaborate further.

"I had a drunk and disorderly case, and it looks like my assault charge is going to go to trial after all," Cassie told me.

I made a sympathetic noise. "Yesterday I moved four squirrels out of a woman's attic. I couldn't get them to relocate to the woods, so now they're in *my* attic." In my living room, actually, but I was reluctant to admit to that.

Cassie wrinkled her nose. "Can't you just tell them to get out?"

My sisters knew my powers. I could communicate with animals, and I could persuade them to do my bidding—usually. Every now and then, like with the squirrels, an animal blocked my attempts at communication and refused to cooperate. I had one other skill, but I refused to break out the nuclear bomb unless a life was on the line. A witch has to have ethical limits after all.

"They're not so bad. I named them Oak, Maple, Pine, and the leader is Hemorrhoid."

Lucien snorted. "You named a squirrel Hemorrhoid?"

"Rhoid for short," I told him. "He's the leader of the crew, and a bit of an asshole. He's really wary of strangers. I hope I can eventually win him over."

"Hard to win someone over when you've named them Hemorrhoid," Cassie commented.

She had a point. "I'm hoping once the weather warms up in the spring, they'll leave my house and head for the woods, but I'm pretty sure they're here for the foreseeable future."

"So they're hanging out in your attic?" Lucien asked.

"That's not too bad other than the noise of them running around."

Crap. Here's where I admitted I was a total softie. "Um, they're living downstairs. They're actually sleeping in my bedroom," I confessed. My sisters already knew I was weird. One more thing wouldn't send me over the weirdness cliff in their eyes mainly because they believed I'd already gone over that edge.

"That's gonna totally kill your sex life," Cassie said.

As if I had a sex life.

"I'm pretty sure Drake is enough of a mood killer on his own." I laughed. "The squirrels *did* ruin a really awesome sexy dream last night though. Actually, it wasn't really their fault. That huge dog-thing was back in my front yard and they were all freaking out about it."

"I totally want to hear about this sexy dream," Sylvie said as she walked into the kitchen.

"Me too." Eshu, her main squeeze, was right behind her. He had a case of beer and handed us each one before he began stacking them in the fridge.

"Please tell me you're not going to take in the stray dog as well," Cassie pleaded as she popped open her beer. "You've already got a vulture and a bunch of squirrels. Soon you'll be sleeping on the couch and all the animals will be in the bed."

"Ooo, Adrienne *could* use some animal action in bed," Sylvie teased.

"Eww." I made a face at her. "I'm not doing it with any animals. Doggy-style, yes. Doggies, no."

"I totally picked the wrong time to come in on this conversation." Glenda made her way through the door carrying a pie.

It smelled heavenly and I smiled, feeling completely at home here in the place I'd grown up, surrounded by my sisters and the demons who were as good as my in-laws at this point. Everyone else arrived and we all were busy preparing the meal and catching up. I didn't say anything further about the squirrels, my dream, or the dog-thing until all the food was in the oven or on the stove and we were relaxing in the living room with beer and chips.

"So tell me about this sexy dream," Sylvie said.

"No, tell us about these squirrels," Ophelia chimed in.

"I want to hear more about the dog." Babylon sighed. "I've always loved dogs."

"You have always loved dogs," Glenda said. "Remember the Schafers' black Lab?"

I reached out and touched Babylon's arm. She'd adored that dog and animated him after his death, but as nice as zombie Rocky was, he wasn't the same as living Rocky. After he'd started to smell, Cassie had convinced our five-year-old youngest sister to let zombie Rocky rest, and gotten Babylon a hamster instead.

"He's huge—like Mastiff huge," I started. "Black fur. It's not fluffy or smooth, but kind of wiry. He likes freeze-dried liver and rib bones—"

"Doesn't every dog?" Hadur laughed.

"True. But this dog had weird shoulders and haunches, and huge white teeth, and glowing red eyes. And a forked tongue."

Lucien frowned. "Sounds like a hellhound, although I don't know why a hellhound would be eating rib bones off your front lawn."

"Those ribs were amazing," I countered. "And there was still a little bit of meat on them too. Any dog, or not-dog, would totally love them."

"What if it *is* a hellhound?" Nash asked. "They're dangerous and vicious."

"I don't think Adrienne needs to fear anything from hell," Lucien drawled. "And the days of rogue hellhounds are long in the past. The last two thousand years, they've been under rule of a skilled demon."

Cassie shrugged. "So one slipped his leash and found his way to Adrienne's? He doesn't sound as if he's a danger to her, but maybe you should let this demon know one of his hounds is roaming around and scavenging for food scraps."

"Maybe Adrienne can catch him next time and keep him in her garage for the demon to retrieve," Babylon said.

"If there is a next time." I thought of the way I'd yelled at the dog-thing and felt ashamed. Poor guy. I hoped he did come back so I could give him more liver treats and apologize for my behavior.

"Enough about the hound, let's hear about the sexy dream," Sylvie chimed in.

"After dinner," Glenda told her. "Xavier and I made some shrimp puffs and we need everyone to taste test them."

My stomach growled. Glenda was an amazing cook, and Xavier wasn't bad in the kitchen either. The pair of them always had these running contests to see who could make a certain dish better, and I loved it when I got to taste test. Both shrimp puff recipes would, no doubt, be amazing, and there would be all sorts of laughing and joking over whose was best.

It was so cute how Glenda and Xavier had this friendly rivalry with each other in the kitchen. And it was especially cute to see them together, hand-in-hand and slipping each other mushy glances. I looked around the room at my sisters and their boyfriends, feeling a pang of jealousy. Being alone never bothered me before, but suddenly with nearly all of my sisters in serious relationships, I felt particularly lonely. It was just me and Babylon that were single out of the family. Babylon didn't seem to be bothered one way or another by her single status, but as Xavier brought in the trays of shrimp puffs and Glenda playfully bumped his hip with hers, I found myself wanting what my sisters had.

The horned dude from my dream appeared in my mind and I almost laughed. Not that. That was sex, and I wanted more than sex. Besides, a sexy horned monster in a dream was a whole lot different than what I was envisioning as a life partner.

We tested the shrimp puffs, deciding that they were both equally good, then we all sat and caught up on each other's lives until the oven buzzer sounded. Everyone sprang into action, putting the final items on the table and helping bring in the food. Once they were all seated and eating, the conversation turned to the situation in Accident.

"How are things going with the werewolf move?" Glenda asked Cassie.

Cassie grimaced. "One step forward, two back. Clinton's group was supposed to be moved out by now, but there's been one problem after another."

"The word in town is the mountain's cursed," Nash chimed in.

Cassie snorted. "There is no curse. I've been up there and the only problem is that we're trying to move a community of werewolves onto a bunch of land that hasn't been occupied in ages."

Bronwyn shook her head. "Even using one of my magic dousing wands to find the best spot to place a well, it took nearly a week from drilling to putting in the pump, to running the main line. And don't get me started on trying to put in a septic field with all those rocks up there."

"The framework for a dozen structures is up, but that's it," Hadur said.

The werewolves were used to living with a bare minimum of modern services. They could move in without electric and with barely cleared roads, but clean water and waste management were deal breakers. Cold weather would be here soon. If Clinton's new territory didn't have more than roughed-in shelters, they'd need to stay where they were until spring. And that would mean more friction between two packs that already had an uneasy peace between them.

"What can we do to help?" Ophelia asked. "I'm no good at construction, but maybe we can fundraise and hire a crew from outside Accident to help get these buildings ready faster?"

Cassie nodded. "It's a good idea, but I'm not sure how much more we can ask the community to contribute. They helped rebuild Dallas's compound and chipped in money for that. They're bound to be feeling kind of tapped out at this point."

"Then let's make it a party," Babylon suggested. "Beer, food, magical fireworks. There have got to be some tasks that can be easily done under supervision, like putting insulation in the walls and nailing up drywall, or running the electrical cord through the walls, or stuff like that."

"We can give it a shot, but I'm not sure how many people will come," Cassie said. "Again, we've been pushing the townsfolk a lot this year to help out on stuff like this."

"Then tell Dallas and Clinton to get all their people over there and get it done," I chimed in. "There's no reason why a few hundred werewolves can't get a dozen structures up and ready in a few weeks. They're stalling."

"They're trying," Cassie insisted. "There was all that rain last week, then the shipment of lumber didn't arrive. Now there's some issue with hornets and a badger. They're tired as well. It's fall, and they're trying to get their harvests in and butcher. Running a crew out to Savior Mountain only to find the lumber didn't arrive is making people less willing to help."

"I know *I'm* feeling less willing to help," Hadur grumbled. "We've all done enough for these werewolves. If they can't get their crap together, then they'll be living in tents this winter. Or they can take Dallas up on his offer and rejoin his pack."

I wondered if that wasn't secretly what Dallas was hoping. It still was an embarrassment to him that his son had absconded with a bunch of his pack to form their own. Clinton's wolves might need to rough it a bit this winter, but it was in nobody's best interests to have them freezing in tents —or abandoning Clinton and adding to the issues still simmering between the two packs.

"I can take care of the hornets and the badger," I volunteered.

"Thanks." Cassie smiled over at me. "Let me know what happens, will you? I don't particularly like displacing wildlife, but I'm eager to get Clinton's pack settled and put all this behind me. Any little roadblock is one roadblock too many."

"I'm up for helping a few days if we decide to do a community barn-raising effort or something," I told her. "I might not have much experience, but I can swing a hammer and operate a saw."

"Me too." Sylvie sighed. "Let's schedule a day and see what we all can get done. If we can at least get rudimentary structures in place before the first frost, I'm counting it a win."

"Okay." Cassie held up her hands. "I'll pick a few days this month and see how those work for everyone. I appreciate you all continuing to chip in here. I know this is getting tiresome."

It was, but we'd put up with werewolf issues since I could remember. For once in my life, I felt like I was seeing the light at the end of the tunnel. A future where Clinton's and Dallas's packs lived in harmony with the town of Accident, following their rules and becoming part of the community, was worth taking a few days off work and getting blisters from running a screw gun for hours at a time.

"Okay." Sylvie stood up. "Let me grab the apple pies out of the oven and then we can hear all about Adrienne's sexy dream while we eat dessert and drink coffee."

Ugh. I'd thought they'd forgotten about that. I got up and followed Sylvie into the kitchen, grabbing mugs and ferrying them out to the table along with the two pots of coffee while my sisters handled clearing off the dirty dishes. This was one of the other downsides of our growing family—more dishes. And the need for a second coffee maker. When there were a dozen people for dinner, one coffee maker just didn't cut it.

It made me all warm and fuzzy inside to think that Cassie went through all this just so we could get together as a family every Sunday night. She'd bought extra plates and silverware, gotten a second coffee maker, doubled her main-dish recipes. And although we all helped with the prep and clean-up, and contributed side dishes and desserts, I'm sure there was still plenty left for Cassie to do once we left for the day.

That's who she was, though. She was the matriarch of our family. She'd been our rock ever since our grandmother had died, and our mother had taken off. She'd been the one who'd raised the younger of us who barely remembered our father and felt Cassie had been more of a mother than the woman who'd given birth to us.

"So." Sylvie motioned for me to sit down and slid a slice of apple pie my way. "Let's hear it."

"It started out as a bit of a nightmare," I confessed. Then I told them all about the horned monster chasing me, how I'd panicked and ran and tried to protect myself from him— until I didn't.

"You know, if you've got a thing about demons, I'd be happy to introduce you to a few," Lucien teased.

Bronwyn rolled her eyes. "Hello. We've all got a thing about demons. Don't hold back on us, Lucien. We've got two single sisters here. Bring out the eligible bachelors."

"No thanks. I'm good." Babylon laughed.

"I think that dream is less about demons and more about Addy embracing what she fears the most," Sylvie chimed in.

"Which is drowning." I shuddered. "I don't care how much you psychoanalyze my dreams, Sylvie, I'm not cave diving. In fact, I'm not scuba diving at all. Ten years of advanced-level swimming and lifeguard lessons have only taught me I'm better off with my feet on solid ground."

She reached out and patted my arm. "I mean loving. You run away and run away, when you should be jumping in with both feet."

"Naked. Sprawled across the bed. Horned dude on top of you," Eshu teased.

"I'm up for that. I just want him gone by morning," I joked.

Actually that was a lie. I wanted someone to stick around. I wanted more than just a booty call. But like Sylvie had said, I was nervous about opening my heart up to someone who would turn out to be a total asshole. No, being alone was better. I had Drake and the squirrels for company. And if I found some hot dude in a bar, then I'd kick my animal companions out of the bedroom for one night. Then go back to my life in the morning.

"Well, I think that was some seriously hot dream," Babylon told me.

"It was, until I was rudely awakened by squirrels," I lamented.

My younger sister chuckled and shook her head. "You seriously need to get laid, Addy. I mean *really* laid, not dream-dude laid."

I snorted. "You're sounding more and more like Sylvie. I

work a lot and I don't exactly meet a lot of guys when I'm getting rid of an ant infestation or removing a pissed-off raccoon from someone's garage. Plus I've got a vulture and four squirrels now living in my bedroom. Kinda kills the mood."

"Kick them out for the night," she said. "Or get a hotel room, or go to his house, or do it in the truck. I mean it, Addy. You need to get out more."

She was right, but somehow after I was done working, the idea of showering, putting on decent clothing and makeup, and going out seemed beyond me. It was all I could do to get clean and put on pajamas most nights.

"Okay, social director. What's going on this week? I promise I'll make it out one night."

One night. Baby steps, right? It was so darned sad. When I'd lived in Accident I'd had a heck of a commute and still managed to get out now and then—at least twice or three times a week. But here I pretty much knew everyone. Outside the wards, I didn't. And there was something that felt strange throwing back a few cold ones with a room full of humans instead of a room full of minotaurs, werewolves, dragons, and trolls.

"Monday is Karaoke night at the bar. Then there's Taco Tuesday with Salsa dancing lessons. Wednesday is wine tasting, and Thursday is craft beer night. Friday and Saturday are kind of hectic, but the bands are always good."

The idea of sitting alone in a packed bar with music blaring didn't sound all that appealing. Actually the idea of sitting alone didn't sound appealing. I wasn't exactly shy, but it was hard to start up a conversation with strangers.

"When are you off work?" I asked Babylon. "Maybe we can go somewhere together and you can introduce me to a few people?"

"Rita and Ralph are hosting a fall party on their farm. Bonfire. Beer. Corn maze. They've got pygmy goats."

"You totally had me at pygmy goats," I told her. "I hate to crash a party, though. I don't know Rita and Ralph at all."

"Silly, you'll be my guest." Babylon reached out and playfully slugged my shoulder. "There's going to be around thirty people there, but I'll probably only know three or four. It's a perfect opportunity for both of us to meet people and connect."

"Thanks." I smiled.

"That's what sisters are for," she said. "And maybe you'll meet someone to boink in the corn—someone more real than a dream demon."

Maybe. But I wasn't counting on it.

CHAPTER 5

ADRIENNE

When I got home, the squirrels nearly tackled me at the door. I'd never gotten this sort of enthusiastic greeting before in my life. What was wrong? Had they run out of nuts to eat? Were they just bored and couldn't manage to manipulate the television remote? Had Timmy fallen in the well?

No, it seemed that the dog-thing had been back prowling around the yard again, and the squirrels were very distraught about it.

"He can't get in," I told them. "First, there's no way he can figure out the door key code, push the buttons, and turn the knob to open the door. Secondly, even if he could manage that, there are magical wards on the house. Besides, I think we've got him all wrong. Just because he's scary-looking doesn't mean he's a bad doggie…or doggie-thing."

Clearly the squirrels had a differing opinion on that.

A hellhound. If Lucien was right, then no wonder the squirrels were afraid. *I'd* been afraid of the dog-thing when I'd first encountered it as well, but I'd quickly changed my mind. Maybe his initial growling and teeth-baring had been because he was scared as well. I'd seen so many hungry strays that acted that way and it took a while for them to trust even me who could communicate with them. He'd clearly loved the liver treats, and I was assuming he was the one who ate the rib bones. He'd come back repeatedly. I was probably the only person who'd been nice to him.

Well, except for yelling at him last night. I did feel bad about that. Poor doggie. Just because he looked scary didn't mean he was that way on the inside. I'd grown up among supernatural creatures who would have terrified any human who set eyes upon them. I needed to not be so judgmental. Heck, less than a month in the human world, and I was already yelling at stray hellhounds to get off my lawn at three in the morning.

Determined to do better, I went and got out a ham bone I'd been saving for soup and took it out to the front lawn. Then I sat and waited.

Orange-red eyes lit up from the woods and I shivered, wondering if this was a good idea or not. I reached out to the animal, asking it to come in close. The orange-red eyes moved, then came out, the darkness revealing a large cat.

"Hey Buster," I greeted our neighborhood feral kitty. "Come get a little ham."

I tore a piece off the bone and held it out as he bounded across the yard toward me. Buster took the meat gently from my fingers and purred as he ate. I waited until he was done to converse further, because Buster felt eating and talking were two things that should not happen at the same time.

After he was done, Buster got really chatty. Evidently a calico two blocks over was in heat and he was planning a midnight serenade in hopes that he could get it on. The guys four doors down hadn't secured the lid on their garbage container last night and Buster had enjoyed some pizza crusts and half a turkey sandwich. The Richardsons had called in an exterminator—sadly not me—and Buster was lamenting the decline in the mouse population over there.

I tossed him another piece of ham and told him that the rest was for the hellhound that had been in my yard last night. He froze, his eyes wide as he looked up at me.

Buster was afraid of the hellhound. He was quite vocal about how it was a monster who only appeared when it was on a hunt. He was positive that the hellhound would kill anyone who got in the way of his prey. Then he would kill his prey and drag them all into a fiery pit of torture.

Cats. They were so dramatic, especially when it came to dogs. I really didn't blame him. I'm sure he'd barely escaped death by dog many times, and being mauled was definitely torture in my opinion. I tossed Buster one more piece of ham, then wished him good luck with the calico as he strolled off.

He wasn't gone five minutes when I heard a rustling in the bushes. Four pairs of red eyes peered at me this time. I gripped the ham bone tight, relaxing when the hellhound stepped out onto my lawn.

I really needed to name him. Or maybe he had a name already. "I've got dinner for you. But first I want to know what I should call you."

He eyed the ham bone and drooled, opening his mouth to reveal those very large, very sharp teeth.

Yeth.

It was a weird name, but I'd respect it. Clearly he liked it if he'd accepted it.

"Okay Yeth, here you go." I tore a piece of ham off the bone and tossed it to him.

Three other hellhounds materialized. Well, not really materialized. They crept out of the brush onto my lawn, but unlike Yeth, these guys didn't seem particularly interested in the ham, or the least bit friendly. Their heads were low, hair raised in a bristle across their shoulders. Teeth even longer and sharper than Yeth's were bared, gleaming white in the porchlight. I suddenly wished I hadn't left Drake inside. Yeah, he was a vulture, but he seemed to be an intimidating figure to these animals.

"Hey pups," I said softly. "Hungry? I've got some ham here." I'd intended on giving it all to Yeth. Hopefully there was enough here for four because I didn't want to know what these guys might do if they didn't get enough food. I wasn't in any danger. I had the skills to protect myself against animals if I needed to. I just didn't want to have to resort to that—I didn't want to ever have to resort to that.

There was a back-and-forth of growls and snarls between the other three and Yeth. I gathered they weren't happy with him accepting ham from me.

"It's not poisoned," I assured them, tossing a few more pieces of ham onto the lawn.

The three swiveled their heads in synchronized precision to stare at the meat. I felt their indecision. Yeth moved in to eat them, and one of the others snapped at him, deciding to take the risk. While he was chewing I tore off more ham and flung it in front of the three, making sure to toss some Yeth's way. Finally they all gave in and I relaxed, throwing ham as they ate so there would always be another piece waiting. There wasn't much more left on the bone, though. And I had no way to divide the bone between four hellhounds. What else did I have in my fridge? Maybe that pack of hard-boiled eggs? I'd definitely have to swing by the grocery in the morning and get some dog food.

Which made me think of something else.

"Are you littermates? Do you all have a home to go to? I can fix up a nice warm spot in the garage for the four of you." I'd thought about letting Yeth inside the house, even though the squirrels were afraid of him, but I didn't know these other three well enough to have them sleeping on my living room couch and rug.

Yeth looked up at me and spoke, eyeing the bone as he chewed on a piece of ham. They weren't littermates, but something close. I couldn't make out exactly what their relationship was. Not quite family. Not quite friends. Packmates? That seemed the closest word to what Yeth was communicating.

Then someone must own them—or had owned them at one time. Perhaps their owner had moved and left them behind. Lucien had said there was a demon in hell who took care of the hounds, but maybe some had slipped their leashes? Run away? Or maybe that demon didn't take care of *all* the hellhounds. Maybe hell had a problem with strays just as we did here.

"Where are you sleeping tonight?" I asked Yeth, since he seemed to be the only one inclined toward communication.

He tilted his head, eyes still on the bone. Evidently they weren't sleeping tonight. No, he'd said they weren't supposed to sleep tonight.

"Nocturnal?" Maybe they slept during the day and hunted for food at night. Poor puppers. Clearly they'd somehow become separated from their home and their demon-Master if they were roaming around all night long, searching for food.

"Tell you what. I'll leave the garage door open enough for you and your buddies to go inside. I'll put some nice soft cushions and blankets for you all, and bowls of water. You'll be safe there. Stay as long as you want, and when I get home from work tomorrow night, I'll have more food for you all."

Yeth looked as if he were about to cry. His bottom lip quivered, and his red, glowing eyes stared up at me soulfully. I reached out a hand and stroked his wiry, coarse fur. He leaned into me, making a little whimper as my fingers found an especially good spot.

Then one of the others growled and Yeth jumped back, sending me a guilty look.

"It's okay Yeth," I whispered. "I'll save the bone for you. It'll be in the garage."

Then I turned to the other three, tearing off the final tiny bits of ham from the bone and throwing them onto the lawn. While they were eating I got up and made my way backwards toward the house.

"Goodnight pups," I said. "Happy hunting, and I'll see you all tomorrow night."

Only Yeth glanced up at me as I walked into my house. I locked the door and set the wards as usual, then remembered that I was still holding a ham bone.

Damn it. I'd promised him and I wasn't going to let the hellhound down.

"Hey Drake," I called to the vulture who was on top of my dining room table, where he could keep an eye on the squirrels. "Come with me to the garage, will you?"

The vulture waddled after me. My garage was pretty much a glorified storage area, which is why I always parked my truck in the driveway. I moved a kayak, bike, two toolboxes, and a dozen Rubbermaid tubs aside then put down four dog pillows that I'd gotten on clearance last year as well as some cheap fleece blankets. The ham bone went on a plastic Thanksgiving platter that was shaped like a turkey, and I filled two large bowls with water. Drake stood guard while I went back into the house and retrieved the package of hard-boiled eggs. Those I placed in a terracotta flowerpot, setting it next to the bone.

There. It seemed reasonably welcoming. I'd get food, treats, some more bowls, and a few toys tomorrow. Hopefully the hellhounds would take advantage of my hospitality and tomorrow night the other three would be less suspicious of me.

Then I'd need to think about what I was going to do with them all. Perhaps I could find some nice people who would be willing to adopt them? If not, I'd be stuck with four giant scary-looking canines, along with four squirrels and a vulture.

a witch. It all made sense now—not that I was going to admit any of that to Yeth.

"She told me to go away," the hellhound whined. "She yelled at me."

If there needed to be any more proof that magic was afoot, Yeth's heartsick sorrow was it. The hellhound was devastated over the woman's anger, and was moping that he'd never get to have liver treats or rib bones again. It was so ridiculous. He was a hellhound. He could go anywhere he wanted, do anything he wanted. Some human yelling at him shouldn't make the slightest bit of difference in his habits, and if he wanted a snack, he was absolutely capable of walking right into someone's house and taking the dinner off their table.

But the witch had clearly cast some sort of spell over him. If I didn't manage to break it, Yeth might end up switching his loyalties and becoming no more than a witch's lapdog. Poor guy.

Although Yeth wasn't my priority, it was *Faust*. I wasn't about to admit that I'd gotten sucked into the witch's dream and been far more interested in sex than in locating my quarry and bringing him back to hell. No, boinking a sexy witch and rescuing Yeth from a horrible fate were not allowed to be at the top of my to-do list.

"Did you locate exactly where you-know-who is?" I began to pace, completely ignoring the soul before me, who was in hell for a multitude of sins including habitually double-dipping in the queso and never returning his library books.

"He's somewhere in the house." Yeth pouted, his thoughts still clearly with the witch. "I believe he was in the bedroom, but I'm not positive. He moves around, but he clearly is staying inside the house—no doubt because of those wards. He knows we can't get through them."

Normally I would have argued that point. A mere witch's spell should have been no hinderance for a demon who was Master of the Hellhounds, but I'd already been seduced by this witch's lurid desires, been rendered helpless against her magic. I wasn't about to downplay the possible effectiveness of those wards. I always enjoyed solving problems with brute force, but it was clear this time I would require another technique.

I could show up in force with my pack of hellhounds and bluff—demand that she hand over Faust, or I'd lay siege to her home. That idea had great appeal, but there was a good chance the witch would call my bluff and I hated to look the fool, especially in front of my hellhounds.

We could wait from a distance until the witch let down her guard or until *he* got tired of hiding out in her house, then make our move. However, I wasn't known for my patience and after searching for Faust for centuries, I didn't want to risk him getting away once again.

I needed more information. I needed to send another hellhound with Yeth this time. Hopefully with two of them, they'd be able to resist her liver treats and remain focused on the job at hand. And if I needed to go visit her dreams a few more times…well, that was a sacrifice I'd be willing to make.

"Go back to her house and see if you can get inside," I instructed Yeth. "Take a few of the other hellhounds with you, that way if you're distracted by liver treats or rib bones, one of the other hounds can go retrieve Faust."

Yeth sniffed, insulted. Still he obeyed, taking Snarl, Barghest, and Vartun with him. I got back to work torturing a pharmaceutical lobbyist and waited for them to return. I wasn't exactly surprised when the three hounds came back to hell without Yeth, or Faust.

"Let me guess, more rib bones?" I asked.

Barghest shook his massive furry head. "Ham."

"It was very tasty ham," Vartun added. "Honey glazed. Lots of fat. I'll definitely go back."

For fuck's sake. I hadn't sent them out to review a new restaurant in town. They were supposed to bring me Faust.

"And Yeth is still there eating ham? Is it too much to hope that he'll remember to get inside her house and get the soul I sent *four* of you to retrieve?"

The three hellhounds cringed. "She promised him the bone," Snarl whined. "I wanted the bone. It's not fair that Yeth gets the ham bone and we don't."

I set aside the nail-studded board I was using on the lobbyist and sighed. There was no way around it. I'd need to go myself, pry Yeth away from his ham bone, and get Faust.

I'd see her again. Was it late enough that she'd be in bed? Naked? Dreaming? Or maybe I could knock and she'd answer the door in some silky negligee, and we head into her bedroom. I imagined all the things we'd do, any thought of Faust completely vanishing from my mind.

"Master?"

I jerked from my reverie and realized I'd been standing

there, staring into the distance while my hellhounds awaited instruction and a soul awaited torturing.

"You hounds continue working on this lobbyist," I told them. "I'm going to go get Yeth and the soul. If I'm not back by the time you're done, then chase the internet trolls around a bit. Make sure you bite them and not just chase them, okay?"

"Got it." Barghest did a little salute with one of his paws, then picked up the board in his mouth. He wouldn't do as good of a job as I would, but it wouldn't be right to leave this soul unpunished while I ran off and got laid—I mean, retrieved an escaped soul.

The witch lived in a modest, one-story house that looked nearly identical to every other house on the block. A huge oak shaded most of her lawn from the moonlight, and a thick hedge defined both sides of her property. A truck sat in the driveway, cages and other equipment stacked neatly in the bed. I eyed the cages, but unlike in the dream, none of them jumped out and attempted to enclose me.

All the lights were off in the house. I reached out with my senses, trying to determine who and what was inside only to encounter a solid wall of very effective wards. They ended abruptly just before the garage, so that's where I headed.

The garage door was open about eighteen inches at the bottom. I knew how loud those suckers were, and didn't want to demean myself by crawling underneath, so I went around the side and found a door.

Unlocked. No wards. I opened it and stepped into the garage only to stop, staring in disgust at my missing hellhound. Yeth was sound asleep, curled up on a stack of towels and pillows as if he were a pampered Pomeranian. The ham bone cradled between his two front paws was absolutely cleaned of all meat. I could see the grooves from his teeth marks from clear across the room. Beside him was a half-drank bowl of water.

As I watched, Yeth snorted. His nose twitched in his sleep and a line of drool dropped from his jowls to his bedding. One of his paws shook in mimicry of running.

Idiot. I should have been angry with him, but I knew how powerful and tempting this witch could be. Besides, it probably was a good thing that he'd remained, just in case Faust attempted a midnight escape.

Leaving my hellhound to his dream, I exited the garage and went back around to the front of the house. Looking around to make sure I wasn't being observed—because even demons don't like having the police called on them—I probed the wards.

Even the best of witches make mistakes, and I was looking for a weak spot, or better yet, a hole that would allow me entry. I could forcibly break my way through, but it would hurt and leave me vulnerable to attack by a rudely awakened, very pissed off witch. The idea of the attack bothered me less than the thought of her being angry. I shook my head, annoyed that I was under this woman's spell just as much as poor Yeth was.

The area along the front of the house was solid, as I'd expected it would be. The wards did seem to get a bit weaker as I went around the side of the house, but not so weak that I wanted to attempt entry. The best point to try was probably going to be where the garage joined the house, but I figured it would be best to check along the back, just in case.

I'd been inside the house—in a dream projection, but still I felt the representation I'd seen was fairly accurate to reality. That meant I knew the layout enough that I paused under the witch's bedroom window.

She'd be in there, asleep, that utilitarian bra that I was beginning to find very sexy draped across the end of the bed or on the dresser. I envisioned her naked, stirring in her sleep as she sensed my presence, reaching down between her legs to touch herself, moaning just a little at the thought of me.

Damn it. An erection was not comfortable in these pants. Besides, I needed to concentrate on getting inside and getting Faust, not a lithe, auburn-haired beauty, her gaze losing focus as an orgasm rolled through her.

I shook my head, cursing under my breath. Then I reached out and checked the ward right under her window.

An electric shock stung my fingers and I felt myself falling as my spirit surged forward. Suddenly I was in the front yard once more, looking up at the witch's house that had inexplicably become six stories high.

What...? A dream. She'd sucked me into a dream clear through the wards. I eyed the window above me and wondered how I'd managed to completely lose control of the situation. I knew how. Thinking about sex did that.

Just then the witch leaned out the window. Glossy hair, pale face, naked shoulders, naked breasts. I stared transfixed.

"You came back!"

She sounded happy to see me. I tried to pull my attention from her breasts, only partially succeeding.

"Let me in," I urged. "I can't get past your wards." Two could play this game. If she was going to enchant me with her magic, then I'd use that to gain entrance to her house. Then I'd grab Faust—right after we had sex, that is.

Her hair unrolled nearly forty feet down the side of the building and onto the ground. I stared at, then looked back up at her breasts, then back down at the hair.

"Climb up," she called out.

I frowned, not understanding how her scalp could possibly hold my weight. Was this some sort of fairy tale reference? I think it might be.

"Won't that hurt?" And did she intend on dismissing the wards on her walls? Because if she didn't, then both of us would wind up in pain.

She sighed and started gathering her hair up. "I guess you're right."

Once her hair was back to its normal length, and my gaze was once more fixed on her breasts, the house morphed into a wagon filled with hay. The witch sat in the middle, fully clothed. Before I could protest her lack of nakedness, she jumped off the wagon, grabbed my face in her hands and kissed me.

It's not my fault one thing led to another and soon we were both naked, sweaty and going at it like rabbits on some very soft grass. I lay there with her on top of me, caressing down the smooth skin of her back to that delectable round ass. My heart still pounded, my mind still swirled, and I'd never felt so alive. Staring up at the strangely indigo sky of her dream, I realized that I just couldn't resist this witch. If I wanted to get Faust I'd have to try to get into her house during the day, when she wasn't there, otherwise I was positive we'd end up in bed, just like we had the last two times I'd attempted to retrieve the soul.

Would she know it was me? If she came home to find her wards broken and Faust gone, would she ask me about it? Because I knew tonight wouldn't be the last time I'd visit her. I was enchanted, wrapped around her witchy little finger. I was hers and if I wasn't here physically, I'd be inserting myself into her dreams as often as I could. There was no way I could ever stay away from this witch.

And that was a problem. If she asked me about Faust, I'd have to tell her. And then she'd never want to see me again— which would destroy me. No, if I were to retrieve the soul, then I needed some way of breaking this spell she had over me.

I didn't want to break this spell she had over me.

The witch stirred in my arms, nuzzling my neck and nipping at my ear. "So, my horned lover, shall we do this again?"

I caught my breath, feeling myself rise, feeling my heart kick into overdrive once more. No, I most definitely didn't want to break the spell she had over me. I needed help. I needed advice. And there was only one demon I knew who had solid, recent experience with witches. I'd need to talk to Lucien.

But first, I was going to get it on one more time with this witch.

Okay, maybe two more times.

CHAPTER 7

ADRIENNE

I brewed an entire pot of coffee the next morning, knowing I was going to need it just to stay awake all day. The squirrels had been a nervous wreck all night, racing all over my room and making all sorts of noise. They even woke Drake up. He wanted to herd them out into the living room and shut the bedroom door, but I felt a bit sorry for them. Just as Rhoid had been afraid of the dog-thing, I knew the other squirrels were too. How many times in their lives had they been chased up a tree by dogs? And kicking them out of the bedroom would only make their anxiety worse. They seemed to get some comfort from my presence, especially Rhoid who kept trying to get under the covers or squeeze under my pillow. With all their noise I probably only got four hours of sleep, and I wasn't the sort of girl who did well on less than her usual eight.

Um, and then there was the sex.

If Saturday's night's dream had been sexy, last night's had been downright orgasmic—as in three or four times orgasmic. That horned, fiery-eyed demon had been back, and although I awoke very satisfied, I was still exhausted.

Wow, I really needed to get laid. Not necessarily a boyfriend, because I wasn't sure I really had the time for an actual relationship. Friends with benefits would sure be nice though. Or just the benefits. If the last two nights were any indication, I was sex starved and desperate for a hot night of mattress aerobics. The dream stuff was great, but how long would that last? What if my unconscious sexual exploits stopped and I began dreaming about boring stuff like roofing repairs, spoiled lettuce in the fridge, my truck breaking down midweek twenty miles from home? I'd had two nights of getting it on. I didn't want it to stop.

So a relationship—preferably a casual one—needed to move up higher on my to-do list. Although that might be a problem when I was sharing my bedroom with a vulture and four squirrels—especially when the squirrels had a habit of chattering all night long and darting around as they looked out the windows.

I think part of the reason they'd been so upset was that there had clearly been at least one canine in the garage last night. I'd peeked when I woke up, and hadn't seen any of them in there, but the bone and the eggs were gone, the water bowls had been drunk from, and the beds and blankets were clearly slept on. Maybe with the food I'd left, they hadn't felt the need to be hunting all night, and had finally gotten some rest. It made me smile to think that I'd done something nice for the poor hounds who'd probably not had anyone be nice to them their entire lives.

Leaving the garage door open a bit, I emptied my fridge of luncheon meat, refilled the water bowls, and straightened the blankets and beds. Then I made sure the ward-stone I'd moved to the doorway into the house was in place, and locked back up again. I felt bad using physical and magical means of securing the house from the hounds, lumping them in with all other intruders, but a girl couldn't be too careful. I could protect myself, but I wouldn't be here all day, and just as I wanted to set safeguards on myself and my belongings when I was sleeping, I felt I should continue to do the same when I was away. Trusting these dog-things with my garage was one thing. I didn't want to come home tonight to find my house had been trashed, and my fridge was empty and tipped over onto the kitchen floor.

That done, I wolfed down some breakfast, poured the extra coffee in a thermos, then began to load up my truck for the trip up to Accident to assist with Clinton's pack's new residence. Hornets meant I might be relocating a nest, so I made sure to pack a long stick with a hook, a bunch of strong twine, and a small saw. The badger might be tricky, so I threw a few humane traps into the back. Badgers weren't usually seen on the east coast, and I was curious why one was living here as well as why he'd taken up residence in one of the mountains that were inside the wards of Accident. They liked grassy meadows, not forested mountains. They liked to dig burrows, which wasn't an easy task in the rocky mountain ground. Admittedly there would be lots of food for them there. Mice, voles, and birds were plentiful as well as insects.

I grabbed a few other things from the house, and got ready to head out. The squirrels dashed past me before I could close the door to the house. I watched in surprise as they jumped into my car and piled into the back seat.

"So did you all change your minds?" I asked them. "Would you rather live in the woods instead of my house?"

I'll admit I was a bit hurt by the idea. They were a total pain in my rear. They'd eaten all my almonds, had kept me awake all night, had interrupted that amazing sex dream Saturday night. I should be relieved that they wanted to ditch me and go live in the woods, but instead I was insulted.

For once, Rhoid was the one who spoke up, telling me that they had every intention of living in my house. They were just afraid to stay there alone, so they were going to accompany me on my travels today.

Now I *was* wishing they were going to live in the woods.

"Guys, get back in the house," I said. "The doors are locked. The windows are locked. There are magical wards in place. It's safe there. It's not safe to come with me today. I've got to relocate a badger. Badgers eat squirrels."

They exchanged a volley of chatter, arguing the best option. Finally Rhoid twitched his tail, letting the others know that he was the one deciding this and that they were going with me. It seemed they had faith in my ability to protect them from hungry badgers as well as anything else that might come to attack them—including the hound.

I didn't have time to argue. "Fine. Just stay out of my way and don't disturb me when I'm driving."

Squirrels evidently have a different idea about what constitutes disturbing someone, because they spent most of the drive asking me what I was going to get them for lunch, if they would have an opportunity to forage while I was doing my work, and if we could all watch movies and eat popcorn again tonight—but not that bird movie again. That was too scary.

We all headed out, making a quick stop at the Starbucks drive-through to get a chai latte for me, a pumpkin scone for Drake, and some vegan bagels for the squirrels. The leaves were just starting to change at the higher elevations and I rolled down the window as we headed past the wards to breathe in the smell of fresh-cut hay, of late berries ripening in the sun, of pine needles carpeting the forests.

Home. Days like this I ached to be back in Accident with my family just down the street. Everything was familiar there. Everyone knew my name.

"I need to just give it time," I said to Drake. "I'll build memories in my new home and neighborhood, and before long it will feel just as comfortable as Accident." Of course, the people down my street might not be thrilled that their new neighbor had squirrels and a vulture living in her house, and a dog-thing eating scraps in her front yard every evening. I'd have to organize a big Halloween party or something and have Glenda cater it. After that, no one would care if I had elephants living in my yard or not. Glenda's food had a way of making everyone happy. Combine that with free beer and all sorts of witchy decorations, and hopefully I'd be accepted into the neighborhood.

The vulture clacked his beak.

"You're right. Babylon has been living outside the wards since she got out of college and she's happy. She made friends and has local hangouts where people know her. Plus it's nice not having to commute two hours each day."

Drake hissed and I laughed.

"Yes, I'm looking forward to that fall party. Should I make pumpkin bars with cream cheese frosting to take?" Glenda was the chef of the family, but I could manage a simple dessert. Besides, it would probably be rude to show up to a party uninvited *and* empty handed.

The vulture eyed me with a nod of his head. If he'd had eyebrows, he would have been wiggling them.

I sighed. "I'd like to meet someone, but right now my priority is making friends and settling into my new home. If the right guy comes along, then awesome. If not, then that's okay."

Heck, at least I had my dream-demon. And if he stopped coming around, there was that vibrator I'd stashed in the back of the drawer in my bedside table.

The squirrels chattered from the backseat and I listened in, amused at their ideas of what an ideal mate for me would be. Seems he should have a very full, bushy tail, a thick gray coat, and be especially skilled at gathering nuts and berries, and evading dogs.

Especially hounds, Rhoid added. *They're very good at tracking you down. If one of them catches your scent, you'd be lucky to get away.*

There was an awed silence from the back seat, then Oak asked if Rhoid had ever had a hound after him.

Many times. One almost caught me, but I managed to hide before he caught my scent.

You should mate with the nice-house lady, Maple told the bigger squirrel. *You have a nice tail and coat, and you are clearly good at evading dogs.*

Rhoid looked up and caught my gaze in the rear-view mirror. *Squirrels don't mate with humans.*

There was something odd in the squeaky words, almost as if Rhoid was wishing for a moment he were human. His emotions and thoughts washed over me and without thinking I deciphered snippets of them. Regret. It had been a long time since he'd felt arms around him. Something about paying a price and choices. I glanced in the mirror again and felt sorry for the little guy. Gray squirrels weren't monogamous by any stretch of the imagination, so if Rhoid was longing for a past relationship, it might have been the one he had with his mother and siblings in the nest. Or perhaps he just wanted to get laid. I'm not sure why he would find that hard to do. The others seemed to regard him as a squirrel worthy of admiration, so I'm sure a female squirrel would as well. Yes, their mating opportunities *were* limited to a few hours twice a year when a female would come into season, but it wasn't as if this area was a squirrel free zone. Rhoid should have been able to get it on with half a dozen females each year, no problem.

Maybe he was picky. Or, like me, maybe he had been too

busy with work and moving to a new home to take the time to go bust a nut.

I turned my attention back to the road as the squirrels continued to offer up suggestions as to my perfect mate. By the time I'd arrived at Savior Mountain, they were in the process of setting me up with some chipmunks they knew.

Savior was just as beautiful as Heartbreak Mountain, but Clinton's pack's new territory had been untended and abandoned to the wildlife for decades. When I was young, I remembered my grandmother saying that a group of elves had once made this mountain their home. Fae were an odd group. Some eagerly participated in the life and community of Accident, while others preferred a more isolated existence. These elves had evidently been the latter. By the time I'd come along, only a handful remained living here, and soon they too left.

No one was required to give notice to leave the town—or to move in for that matter. All supernaturals were welcome as long as they followed some basic rules and respected the other beings that made this place their home. This was meant to be a sanctuary—and for some, that sanctuary was only needed on a temporary basis. Grandmother had told us the elves had gone back to their fae home, and although that was absolutely fine, I'd always been sad about it. Why had they left? Didn't they feel welcome here? Didn't they know that life in Accident was better than life anywhere else?

Maybe they'd just gotten tired of a two-hour-per-day commute, and needed to move closer to where they worked.

I put the truck in four-wheel drive, then slowly made my way up the road to where Clinton was building his compound. Although several vehicles had been up here before, it was still rough going. There were brambles and bushes that reached out to scratch along the side of my truck. Saplings had sprouted mid-road, and although the bigger ones had been hacked down, smaller ones were still there to bend as I drove over them. I carefully edged around washed out sections and boulders only to come to a stop in front of a giant downed tree.

"Guess we'll have to go on foot," I told the others. I was assuming the tree had recently fallen, otherwise one of Clinton's pack would have moved it. Although it *was* a bit large for one werewolf to manage on his own. Perhaps someone had noticed it and gone back for help?

Either way, I had clients to see this afternoon and didn't have time to wait around for werewolves to come back and move a tree. Getting out of my truck, I grabbed one of the cages in the back, slung my bag over my shoulder, and eyed the thick oak trunk that lay across the road.

The squirrels and Drake had no problem getting over to the other side, but the tree was thick enough that trying to climb up and over it wouldn't be an easy task. I walked around to the right, but the tree had fallen into a mess of brambles that looked a whole lot less fun than crawling over a thick trunk.

Walking around to the left, I saw the massive, dirt-encrusted root ball from where the tree had come up from the ground. Thankfully that area was relatively clear, and I made my way past some sticker bushes and vines to round the fallen tree.

I didn't have the same affinity toward trees as I did animals, but I'd spent enough time in the woods growing up that I wondered why this tree had toppled. Had some infection taken out the root system? A blight of some sort? It was a shame that a tree would grow so huge and strong only to be taken down by mold or fungus.

On the other side I saw that a huge crack split the tree nearly straight up the middle. Inside, the core was black and rotted, a sickening sweet smell oozing out from the center. I put my arm over my nose and mouth, but before I could turn away I saw something glinting along the edge of the split.

Moving closer, I knelt down and picked it up, holding my breath to keep from gagging at the smell.

It was a bone. Probably the remnant of some animal's dinner that they'd been keeping in this split in the tree, although what carnivore would find the smell pleasant enough to store their food there was beyond me.

I shoved the bone in my pocket and hurried back down the road toward Clinton's compound. It would be interesting to identify what sort of animal had met their end here and give the bone a proper burial. Later.

Once I was done evicting some hornets and a badger, later.

It was only a mile hike into the rudimentary compound, but it took longer than usual due to the incline and my lack of physical fitness. Heck, I'd only moved away a month ago and I was already huffing and puffing going up a mountain road? I needed less time in front of the television with popcorn and more time jogging or lifting at the gym. Just when I was wishing I'd waited for some werewolves to come along and move that fallen tree, I saw the compound.

It wasn't all that pretty, but in the spring the wildflowers and grasses would grow over the areas where the trees had been cleared and the well and septic put in, and it would look like a beautiful meadow dotted with frame homes. Right now it was a rocky, muddy mess with torn-up trees off to the side where the backhoe had pushed them. The houses were pristine pine lumber and plywood sheets, the roofing trusses covered with bright blue tarps. I assumed in addition to running pipes and wires, the werewolves would be getting the roof and shingles on, then the doors and windows. As Cassie had said, winter was fast approaching, and Clinton and his pack really needed to be off Heartbreak

Mountain before the first frost, and before Dallas lost his patience.

But before they did that, I needed to relocate the hornets who were making roofing work a nightmare for the were-wolves. And a badger—although why the werewolves couldn't deal with one little badger, I didn't know. I closed my eyes and extended my awareness. My four squirrels were arguing with another two about trespassing and territory rights. Drake was staring at a werewolf's discarded lunch remains, wondering why humans felt the need to cook their meat. Three does were grazing nearby, very aware of my presence. Birds. Insects.

Hornets. I opened my eyes and walked over to one of the far houses that had been built under a huge sycamore tree at the end of the clearing. There, up on a high limb, was one of the biggest hornet's nests I'd ever seen.

There was no way I'd be able to reach that nest with my collapsible pole, even if I climbed up on the roof trusses of the house. I wasn't even sure I'd be able to carry that nest somewhere else, it was so huge. I could ask the hornets to leave.

I could do more than ask them, but I refused to do that. It wasn't right to take an animal's will. No, I'd *ask*. I'd reason. And hopefully we could come to an understanding because if the werewolves continued to get stung, then their next step would be to break out the poison.

And none of us wanted that. Well, the hornets and I didn't want that. I'm pretty sure no one beyond me cared about hornets. I called up to them, but none responded, so I looked around until I found a good-sized ladder, propped it against the house, and climbed as high as I dared.

"Hello! Hornets?"

A few emerged from the nest, buzzing around the open-ing. I tried to explain the situation to them, but they were more concerned about dwindling food supplies and the threat of predation by birds. After some back and forth, I managed to convince them that the werewolves working on this house were not a threat, and promised that the workers would not come within six feet of their nest.

I made my way carefully down the ladder, nearly jumping out of my skin when a pair of hands grabbed my waist and eased me down.

"Shit, Clinton! You nearly scared me half to death!" I scolded the werewolf alpha. As big and brawny as they were, werewolves were pretty darned light on their feet. I hadn't even heard him approach.

"Sorry." The werewolf grinned sheepishly. "Saw your truck by the downed tree and came to see if you needed a hand."

"I just finished dealing with your hornet problem." I gestured toward the nest. "Tell everyone to stay at least six feet from the nest and they'll leave you alone. Unless you start swatting at them, that is."

Clinton scowled. "Can't you smoke them to sleep and move the nest? I don't trust those things one bit. Yesterday I got stung, and I gotta say it was the most painful experience of my life. I've been stabbed, shot, hit over the head with a fire hydrant, and nothing hurt like that damned hornet sting."

I grimaced, thankful that I'd never experienced a hornet sting. "They can't vacate this late in the year, and that nest is too big and too high for me to move it. They're really not aggressive. It's only when they're protecting their nest or they're threatened that they attack. Otherwise they're very peaceful creatures."

"Peaceful my ass." The werewolf glared up at the nest. "Darla and Billy are supposed to live here along with their three pups, Billy's two brothers and Darla's mother. None of them wants to get stung taking out the trash or sittin' on their porch. I'm thinking we should just spray them."

I did not want him thinking that was a solution. "You're gonna spray that poison and have it dripping down on the ground where three pups are going to be playing?"

Clinton wrinkled his brow in worry, looking at the area under the nest. "Okay, but nobody wants to be living under a hornet's nest. Nobody."

I sighed and motioned for him to lean down closer to me. "Look," I whispered. "Don't let them know, but come November, they'll all be dead except for the queen. She'll hibernate elsewhere, and won't use the old nest next year. Once winter sets in, we can take the nest down. I'll find the queen and I'll move her to the other side of the mountain while she's hibernating. When she wakes come spring, she'll start a new nest somewhere far away from your settlement."

Clinton jerked upright, his eyes wide. "They're all gonna—"

I reached up to slap a hand over his mouth. "Don't say it. They don't need to know that. It's just that there's no food come winter, and…you know. So just tell Darla and the others that if they're polite and respectful for a few months, then everything will work out. Both your pack and the hornets will be happy."

"'Cept for the dead ones," Clinton muttered under his breath.

I glared at him. "But you agree? I made a deal that you wouldn't bother them and they wouldn't bother you."

He huffed out a breath. "Fine. As the alpha of my pack, I will honor the terms of your agreement with the hornets. Now, how about the badger?"

"That's next on my list." I moved the ladder to the ground. "So where is this badger? I can't sense him anywhere near here."

Clinton shot me a narrowed side-eye look. "You can sense animals? I thought you could just talk to them."

The werewolves had always been a little afraid of me and my abilities. Correction, a *lot* afraid. Ever since I was a kid they'd been worried I could do some sort of mind control magic and that my abilities towards animals would also extend to them in their wolf form—and possibly extend to them in their non-wolf form. I'd never tried my magic on the shifters in Accident. It had always seemed rude and intrusive to even attempt it. So I honestly didn't know if I could influence them or not.

"I *can* sense animals, but only within thirty or forty feet of me. It's not always accurate either. If they're sleeping or hibernating, or underwater then I can't sense them. I need their mental activity to know they're nearby, so that means it doesn't work on all animals, and I only pick up a presence about seventy percent of the time." It was still better than accidentally walking into an occupied bear den, or unknowingly stepping on a ground nest of yellow jackets.

"The badger's got a den over this way." Clinton turned and I followed him across the muddy compound.

Of course, as a nocturnal animal, I wasn't likely to be sensing any badgers in the area. They were pretty reclusive, and weren't common to this area of the country at all, so I was actually doubting that the werewolves had a badger problem at all. It probably was a skunk. Or a mink.

Imagine my surprise when Clinton pointed out a burrow that did, in fact, hold a sleeping badger. He wasn't deep in the sett, and I could see his wedge-shaped body and a paw with some impressively long claws only about a foot inside the tunnel.

"So what exactly is your problem with this guy?" They were omnivorous, eating worms, grubs, insects and small mammals, along with fruit and roots. None of that would make them competitors for prey in the eyes of the were-wolves. They were fierce when cornered, but tended to avoid contact and kept to themselves.

"He sprayed some musky shit on Bruce the other night. His wife made him take three baths in tomato juice and sleep outside on the porch." Clinton laughed. "Sleeping on the porch didn't bother Bruce nearly as much as taking three baths. That guy thinks once a week is too much. Three in one night? Thought he was going to die over there from all he was complaining."

I stood up. "And what exactly did Bruce do to get sprayed?"

Clinton shrugged. "Heck if I know. Look, I get that you're on the side of these animals, Adrienne, but this is gonna be our new home. I need my pack to feel comfortable here, or they'll start thinking things might be better with Dallas. That means the hornets and the badger got to go. Now, I respect you witches and all you've done for me and my kind here in Accident. That's why I came to Cassie and didn't take these things into my own hands. But I can't have hornets stinging folk. And I can't have badgers spraying Bruce."

I understood, but I wanted to hear this badger's side of the story. And I wasn't inclined to go kicking him out of his home just because he sprayed some werewolf. This was Acci-dent, and here we all tried to get along. I know I was the only one who included animals in that mandate, but it was impor-tant to me that I didn't evict a creature when there was another solution at hand.

Which was odd given that outside the wards, in the world of humans, evicting animals was exactly what I did. Still, I never displaced bats or rodents when they had young in a nest, and I always made sure to provide an alternate home for them. I'd put bat boxes, bird houses, and squirrel boxes all over the place. I'd relocated insect nests and made sure animals I moved had plenty of food to get them started in their new location. I just wanted everyone to get along. I wanted a win-win situation.

So I wasn't going to evict a reclusive badger living a hundred yards from the werewolf compound just because some wolf named Bruce with poor personal hygiene had gotten himself sprayed.

I made Clinton go back to the compound, then I knelt by the sett once more, hoping this badger wasn't overly grumpy when awakened.

"Mr. Badger? I'm so sorry to disturb you during your sleep, but I need to discuss something with you. It's about the incident the other night with a werewolf?"

The furry form grumbled then twitched, his long claws scratching along the dirt.

"Badger, I know it's early for you to awaken, but I need to talk with you."

Go away.

I recoiled, not because of fear, but because of shock. My gift allowed me to communicate with animals. It also allowed me to communicate with shifters in their animal form. Thus I knew very well that a wolf expressed himself in a far different manner than a werewolf on four legs.

This wasn't a badger. At least it wasn't a badger-badger. It was a werebadger.

Shifters continued to retain some of their animal traits in their human form, so although this guy probably preferred to stay up all night and sleep all day, he was perfectly capable of getting his ass up and out of his sett to talk to me.

"Hey! You!" I shouted. "I'm Adrienne Perkins, a witch of Accident. Get out of there and talk to me right now or I'll have you tossed outside the wards and banished."

The werebadger rolled over and opened an eye. He might be here under the radar, keeping his presence a secret by hiding out in his animal form, but I was sure he knew the rules and regulations of being in Accident. Otherwise he wouldn't be here when badgers typically weren't found on the east coast.

Slowly he made his way out of the tunnel. I backed up to give him room and he shook the dirt off his fur, stretching a bit before transforming into his human form.

A naked human form.

I was used to seeing naked shifters, naked fae, and the occasional naked human, but I didn't know this guy and he was...well, he was fairly impressive in the reproductive organ department.

I tried not to stare. "A werewolf pack is taking possession of this section of the mountain, and the other night you sprayed one of them."

He wiggled his hips making things bounce around. "He deserved it, the wanker. Guy was poking at me with a bloody stick."

I had no idea why a man who shifted into an American Badger was speaking with a British accent, but it wasn't the weirdest thing I'd ever encountered in my life, so I let it go.

"Did you identify yourself as a shifter?" I'm sure Bruce thought he smelled funny, but given that we don't have badgers here, he probably thought this shifter was just a weird animal—a weird threatening animal with huge claws.

"I shouldn't have to shift forms just because that fool didn't recognize me. It's rude to poke someone with a stick, whether they're an animal or a shifter."

I agreed with that. And wouldn't Bruce be mortified to realize he was actually annoying another shifter—well, annoying not-on-purpose. Bruce and many of the other werewolves did plenty of annoying on purpose.

"You're going to have a hard time living in your badger form this close to a werewolf compound," I warned him. "Be prepared for a lot of them to mistaken you for a non-shifter."

"Then they better be prepared to smell like old gym socks for a few days," he replied smugly. "I was here first and I'm not moving."

He had a point. And if we'd known he'd dug a sett here, or that there was a werebadger living inside the wards, we would have let Clinton know to choose land farther away.

"Officially you *weren't* here." He started to speak and I held up a finger—not my middle one because I'm polite. "We don't require anyone to announce their presence or register or anything, but this is exactly what happens when we have supernatural beings living here that we don't know about."

"I've been here three months," he complained. "The food supply is good. I've already dug my sett—and can I tell you how unpleasant it is to dig with all the rocks in the ground here? Thought I was going to need a demolition hammer. Plus winter is right around the corner. I'm not moving."

"Then you need to learn to get along with the were-wolves. Be a good neighbor. Don't spray them, and let them know you're a shifter if you encounter them."

He reached down to scratch his balls and muttered something about territory and people waking him up in the middle of the day.

"How much territory do you need?" I asked, forcing my eyes up to his face. "I can't do much about the noise with the compound so close and the construction going on, but perhaps you can sleep farther back in your sett so it doesn't disturb you?"

He scowled. "During the day I'd like it if everyone can keep to their side of the stream. At night too, but I like to head out to where they're digging that road to find some dinner, so I probably won't be here at night."

I nodded. "I'll have the werewolves flag your area,

although they may need to use the stream itself. As for dinner, they won't be eating the same things you are, so you don't need to worry about them taking your prey."

Small mammals made up a good proportion of an actual wolf's prey, but werewolves tended to do their shopping at the supermarket or rely upon domesticated animals and farming, and when they were in their animal form, they were hunting larger prey.

He nodded, then looked over to the compound. Something about the expression on his face gave me an idea.

"Good neighbors socialize," I offered. "Perhaps the werewolves can include you in the occasional dinner. They put on quite a barbeque."

He thought about it a moment then nodded. "Okay. But only occasional. I don't like being human very often. And I'm not sure they'd want me to reciprocate unless wolves like eating earthworms."

I doubted that. "No, it's only right for them to play the hosts since there are so many of them and only one of you."

"Good. I'm Trap."

He stuck out a hand and I shook it with mine before I could realize it was the same hand he'd been scratching his balls with. Ewww. I hoped I still had some sanitizing wipes in the truck.

"Adrienne Perkins. You can call me Addy."

He grinned. "Well Addy, if you don't mind I'd like to get back to my bed. Unless you'd like to join me, that is."

"Doubt I'd fit." I couldn't help but grin. "My witch powers don't include transforming into an animal."

He nodded. "Just talking to them, then? Got it. Good to meet you. Come over sometimes for earthworms."

Before I could reply, he was back in his badger form, waddling his wedge-shaped body into the tunnel and curling up into a furry ball.

CHAPTER 8

TYPHON

*Y*eth had finally slinked into hell early morning, just before the sun would have been rising at the witch's house. I couldn't blame him for being just as under that witch's spell as I was, but I still took the opportunity to chew him out. He'd failed to capture Faust, was under the spell of honey-smoked ham, and had spent the night curled up in her garage, cuddling a ham bone and eating hard-boiled eggs.

I didn't mention that I'd spent the night boinking that same witch in her dreams, also failing to capture Faust. Yeth didn't need to know about my failings.

Instead I headed in to see the son of Satan, my head completely occupied by memories of last night. Lucien greeted me at the door of a large house that looked like it had been cobbled together a section at a time over the last few centuries. Inside was human and homey with comfortable seating and a table that looked big enough to hold a board meeting. I followed the other demon into the kitchen where we sat at a little metal table and drank coffee.

"So…this is your home." For a reason most of hell found

bizarre, Lucien was living here among the humans. He'd come for vacation earlier this year and never returned. Rumors quickly flew through the fiery depths that he'd found a witch to bond with. I originally hadn't paid attention to the gossip. It wasn't my business who the prince was screwing. I normally tried to avoid the guy as much as I could, but with his father dealing with some VIP arrivals in hell I was temporarily reporting to his spawn.

And that worked to my advantage. If the rumors were true, then Lucien knew about witches. He knew how tricky and enchanting they were. He could help me with my little problem. He could help me retrieve Faust, and somehow hopefully manage to do it without losing the witch I was falling for.

What an idiot. I didn't even know her name and I was falling for her? Sheesh.

Lucien shrugged, looking a bit embarrassed. "It's Cassie's. She grew up here. Her family's lived here since they founded the town. I tried to get her to move somewhere more stately, but she refused."

She refused. And Lucien knuckled under and moved in. The coffee churned in my stomach as I thought about the son of Satan, a powerful demon, becoming a doormat to a witch.

"It wasn't a battle worth fighting," Lucien went on. "Outside of my desire to live in a house that mirrored my station, I have no complaints. It's centrally located, and location really is everything."

What was he talking about? He worked in hell. He teleported. And I got the impression this wasn't some posh address as far as human standards went. We were in some podunk town in a valley surrounded by mountains.

"And Cassie loves it. She'd be so unhappy if she had to live somewhere else."

Ah. That I understood. My mind wandered back to last night, to the sound of my witch's laugh, the beauty of her smile. The thought of her being unhappy nearly gave me a panic attack of anxiety.

"What is it like?" I asked him. "Being mated to a witch, that is. Did she cast a spell upon you to lure you in?"

Lucien chuckled. "It feels like that some days. I'll admit there was an immediate attraction, but looking back I doubt it was magic on her part. In fact, she was really annoyed with me at first. She didn't believe I was a demon. She thought I was a human who'd wandered into town, gotten into a fight with a few werewolves, and ended up in jail."

I scooted my chair even closer and leaned in. "Go on."

The other demon glanced around before speaking. "I love *her*—not just the sex. She's strong, smart, and sassy. She's got a temper to rival any demon in hell. She's fiercely loyal and protective. She's funny. She makes me laugh. I haven't laughed this much in centuries. We're bonded. That means both of us are stronger together than we are alone. I give her magic a boost, and she enhances my powers—all through our bond."

I sat back. Wow. "What if you do something and she doesn't like it?"

Lucien grimaced. "There's a huge fight and it usually includes setting things on fire and a whole lot of yelling. The makeup sex is totally worth it, though."

That decided it right there. This witch who was sheltering Faust may have put a spell on me, but I still wanted her—and I wanted the sort of relationship Lucien had without all the fire and yelling, that is. Makeup sex. Hmmm. I'd break through her wards, grab Faust, then endure a big fight. I didn't like the idea of fighting, but as long as there would be makeup sex at the end of it, I'd get through it.

"She forgives you, right?" I asked, a little worried about

this plan of mine. "After all the yelling and fire and the makeup sex, things go back to normal? She doesn't refuse to see you ever again or vow to never rest until she disembowels you or something?"

"You need to make sure the makeup sex is really good." Lucien emphasized his point with a raised index finger. "If you did something really bad, then you might need to bring her flowers or cook her dinner, or even grovel a little."

"*Grovel?*" Lucien *groveled?* The son of Satan *groveled?*

"Just a little." He made a pinch motion with his thumb and index finger. "Happy witch, happy life."

Break through the wards. Steal Faust and return him to hell. Come back and endure the yelling and fire. Enjoy the makeup sex, but ensure my performance is top notch. Grovel. I really didn't like the last one, but I'd do it if it meant the witch forgave me.

"So, what do you need to discuss this morning?" Lucien leaned back in his chair, cradling his coffee mug in his hands, the picture of an executive from hell.

"He's here," I told the other demon. "We've managed to finally locate Faust."

"Faust? Here? Where?" The prince looked confused as if he expected the man to be hiding behind the stove or in the pantry.

"*Here.*" I gave the pronoun lots of emphasis. "He's about twenty miles from this town."

"You've found Faust?" Lucien asked.

I winced, wondering if bedding a witch had addled his brains. Was this what I had to look forward to?

"Yes. We know his location, but haven't yet laid eyes on him. The man was tricky when he was alive, and I'm willing to bet he's learned a thing or two since his escape."

"So you know his general location? As in a few square miles?" Lucien's expression was hopeful. "Do you honestly think we might finally be able to retrieve this bastard and drag him back to hell where he belongs?"

Shit, I hoped so. "He's in a house. He's *inside* the house, but he could be hiding anywhere inside. I've verified this personally. My hellhounds have felt his presence there, and so have I."

Lucien frowned. "Then what's the problem? It's a house. Search it. Tear it down. Set it on fire and wait for him to come out. Why haven't you hauled him back to hell yet?"

I clenched my teeth, unwilling to admit that we'd been trying with no success—that *I'd* been trying with no success.

"There are some...difficulties in that. First, he's cagey and we don't want to tip him off that we've discovered his whereabouts only to have him vanish on us. I'd like your permission to send my pack to surround the house and remain there until he can be retrieved. Secondly, there are some fairly strong wards around the house, and the dwelling is in a neighborhood. Breaking them would bring attention from the humans."

There was a time when I didn't have to ask permission to send my pack of hellhounds to scorch the earth and shred every living thing in their path. The world had changed though—for the worse in my opinion.

"Why can't your hellhounds retrieve him?" Lucien asked. "Just snatch him on his way to the grocery store if there's a problem getting into the house."

"We haven't seen him leave the house. If I can have the hellhounds do a twenty-four-hour surveillance, we might be able to grab him if he leaves, but that means the humans are going to see a pack of hounds on a stakeout. And if we go in to forcibly retrieve him...well the humans are going to notice that as well."

I had a plan. I was ready to move. But I didn't want to have the upper management of hell coming down on my head because I freaked out a whole bunch of humans and possibly risked breaching our stealth contract with heaven.

"You and your hounds can break into one human's house to retrieve Faust." Lucien rolled his eyes. "We'll take care of any fallout. Just go get him."

There was my permission, but if thousands of years in hell had taught me anything, it was to make sure all the risks had been laid on the table, and that I had informed consent to proceed.

"We haven't been able to observe him inside the dwelling, but he appears to be living with a woman and using magic to keep the hellhounds outside. There are wards," I reminded Lucien. "They're powerful enough that smashing through them would do significant damage to the house, and cause quite a lot of noise."

"The longer Faust is free, the more we look like fools." Lucien shook his head. "We should have secured him better once we'd dragged him into hell. It's not your fault, Typhon. He just wasn't an appropriate soul for your level and punishment methods."

I bristled. Even though the prince might not blame me, I blamed myself. I'd lost a soul. Well, not *lost* per se, but had one escape me. Yes, Faust had help getting out of hell. Yes, he was rumored to be capable of magic and he'd managed to live for centuries, slipping away from every reaper who'd been sent to snag his soul. I should have realized he'd need special precautions—and special punishments.

I needed to do what I needed to do, regardless of how the consequences of that might pain me. There was no escaping this. I'd need to use my hellhounds to guard the residence, then break through the wards and go in myself to retrieve him. I was strong enough to break through the wards, strong enough to resist the witch's spell. I'd go in, grab Faust by his scrawny neck, and drag him back to hell.

And then the witch would hate me. No more sexy dream time. No more nothing. I needed to ensure the makeup sex was truly exemplary, or I'd spend the rest of my life mourning her loss.

"I'm going to send Abraxas in to take care of it," Lucien decided. "There's no need for you or the hellhounds to get involved. I appreciate your tracking him down, but Abraxas is better suited to bring Faust back to hell."

I nearly growled. The thought of that asshole demon facing *my* witch made me want to strangle someone. And the humiliation… Faust had escaped from *my* level of hell. Sending in another to retrieve him was an insult.

"My Prince, there's no need to interrupt Abraxas from his very important duties. I can handle this myself. Me and my hellhounds."

Lucien waved a hand. "No, you're right. I don't like the idea of sending in your pack. They poop all over the neighborhood. People complain. Next thing you know the police are called—or worse, animal control."

"Animal control?" Last I'd heard that was a local human government group that didn't do much beyond scraping dead animals off the roads and picking up lost kittens.

Lucien scowled. "Yes, animal control. They'll take one look at your hellhounds then they'll call in…well, they'll call in a contractor, and it'll get back to someone I don't want it to get back to. If *she* hears, she'll want to know what's going on and she won't be happy."

I was totally lost. "*She* won't be happy about us retrieving Faust?"

"No, she won't be happy about hellhounds prowling around a human neighborhood twenty miles outside of Accident."

I was still lost, but I nodded as if I knew what in the hell the prince was talking about. "So I'll go in without the hellhounds." It would be difficult. Faust might slip away while I was battling the witch—or doing other things with the witch. Having my hellhounds there would ensure the fiend didn't slip out the back door and vanish for another few centuries.

Lucien nodded. "Go ahead, but I'm still putting Abraxas on this as backup. I don't want this guy getting away again. Granddad's been busting my father's chops over this for centuries now."

I winced. "Don't worry. This time we'll get him." And I'd make sure *I* was the one bringing Faust in—not that slime-nosed, web-footed Abraxas.

Leaving the house where Lucien had set up residence with his witch, I wandered down the street, musing on how I might accomplish my goal without the hounds. In the time I would need to forcibly break through the wards, Faust could slip away. Plus there was the witch to deal with. I needed a way to get into the house with stealth and to do it when the witch wasn't at home. Or I needed a way to quickly neutralize the witch and grab Faust before he got away.

Looking up, I realized my walk had taken me outside of this strange town and on a road that headed toward the mountains. A rustic establishment stood to my right with a sign proclaiming it to be a bar and pub. Pistol Pete's.

I was feeling a bit hungry here in a physical form, and alcohol was known to have been the inspiration for many a daring plan. With that in mind, I headed in and sat at the end of the bar. That's when I noticed that nearly every being inside Pistol Pete's was not human.

A troll and a werewolf were holding hands and giggling at a table. A bleary-eyed dragon sat mid-floor, knocking back a shot of tequila. Three fairies were flirting with a satyr over by the dance floor. A bear shifter, a minotaur, and a witch were eating lunch at the bar.

Wait.

Not just any witch. This was *my* witch. I caught my breath, every cell in my body igniting at the sight of her. She was even more beautiful in the flesh than she'd been in her dream. Her auburn hair looked flame-kissed in the ambient lighting. Her eyes were a lighter brown than I'd thought, and her figure was just as enticing clothed as it had been naked.

I couldn't accost her here, not with a building full of creatures that could collectively kick my ass. Plus, I'd felt oddly weakened since I'd entered this town. I had no doubt that if I got her back to my bed—I mean, my circle of hell—I could find out all of Faust's plans, his location, and how to slip through the wards to grab him. I just had to somehow snatch her up without being pummeled by bear shifters and having a dragon fry me to a crisp.

She looked over and caught me staring, a blush staining her cheeks. Then she smiled, grabbed her glass of water, and made her way over to me.

"Figures you'd move into town after I left," she said, sliding into the seat beside me. "You're clearly not a shifter or a vampire. Fae? Elemental?"

"I'm the Master of the Hounds," I told her. It seemed more impressive than just saying I was a demon, and I wanted to impress this woman who'd woven her magic around me in both her dream and now in this bar.

"Fae then?" She tilted her head and regarded me with a quizzical look. "So you're in charge of the Night Hunt?"

I had no idea what she was talking about, but the hellhounds did hunt for souls, so I nodded. "And you're a witch."

She blushed again, her smile revealing the most entrancing dimples I'd ever seen.

"Yes. Adrienne Perkins. Call me Addy." She held out her hand.

"Typhon." I took her hand and raised it to my lips, feeling

an electric spark shoot through me at the softness of her skin.

She sucked in a breath, her gaze on my mouth. "Typhon. Ty. That's a nice name."

I was so damned hard. All thoughts of Faust had left my brain, replaced by visions of her naked underneath me, calling my name with that soft, breathless voice.

"What…um, what are you doing tonight, Ty?"

That blush was just as sexy as her dimple.

"Spending it with you." Who knew I could be so smooth? I was rather proud of myself for that response.

"Good." The dimple made another appearance. "And what exactly are we doing? Dinner? Dancing? Putt-putt? Oooo, can I meet your dogs? I love animals. I mean, I really really love animals. They're my thing."

She clearly didn't know. She hadn't connected me with the demon in her dreams. She didn't know it was my hounds that had been eating her liver treats, rib bones, and leftover ham.

And "Putt-putt?" What in the hell was that?

"Awesome! Putt-putt it is. When should we meet? Six? Seven?"

"Six?" I felt totally off balance, realizing that I'd lost any sense of what was going on in this conversation. "I don't know where the putt-putt is. Should I pick you up?" I'd need to steal a car, but that was no big deal. Hmm, I should make it a really nice car. Not too ostentatious because I didn't want to arouse suspicions. No, I wanted to arouse other things. A German sedan? Restored classic muscle car? Sporty two-seater?

She grabbed a napkin, then pulled a pen from her purse and wrote down an address before shoving it into my hand. "Pick me up at six. Call or text me if you have any trouble finding the house. Oh, and don't mind the vulture and the squirrels. And the big dog that might be in the garage or in the front yard."

The witch slid off her seat and took a step into me, pressing her lips against my cheek for a quick kiss. For a second I was completely immobilized. The warmth of her soft body against mine, nestled between my legs as she leaned in. The aroma of peppermint and lavender as her auburn hair brushed against my face. The nearly painful response of my body to her lips on my cheek.

By the time I'd recovered my senses, she'd left. I looked down at the address that I already knew on the napkin and the phone number, then tucked it into my jacket pocket.

"Dude, you are so going to get some tonight." The bear shifter saluted me with his beer.

"Yeah, Addy isn't shy about going for what she wants." The minotaur nodded in respect. "Kudos, man. You're golden as long as you don't fuck this one up."

Sadly, I was going to fuck this one up. I was going to let her seduce me, let her bring me inside of the wards of her house, then betray her to grab Faust and haul him back to hell. Part of me wanted to have sex before I did that, but I wasn't *that* much of a demon.

CHAPTER 9

ADRIENNE

I skipped into Cassie's office, feeling as if I were walking on clouds. I'd wanted to see her before heading to my next appointment, to let her know the resolution on the hornet situation as well as what was happening with the werebadger.

And about my date. Oooo, I had a date with a totally hot guy I'd met at Pistol Pete's of all places. I'd been having lunch there after dropping the squirrels and Drake off at the firehouse to entertain Ophelia, and he'd walked in. Tall, dark, and handsome. And he liked dogs.

"Hey!" I plopped down in the chair across from my sister and told her all about the hornets and the badger, wondering if I should tell her about my date or not. Probably not. As excited as I was, Cassie would be downright ecstatic. And she'd get her hopes up. I was optimistic, but if this guy turned out to be a total douchebag, I didn't want to have to explain all that to Cassie.

"So this werebadger has been there for months?" Cassie shook her head. "It's not like any of us have gone up there much since the elves left. It's all overgrown and wild. I guess if he wanted to live an isolated life where he could burrow up in his animal form for a few years, Savior Mountain would be the place to go."

"Except it's not going to be an isolated life with a rancorous werewolf compound practically on his doorstep." I shrugged. "He doesn't want to move. Says it's a pain digging a sett in that rocky ground. He'd rather just set boundaries with the werewolves and learn to deal with neighbors. Actually I got the idea he was kind of intrigued by my suggestion of Clinton's pack hosting him for an occasional dinner. I think he's lonely but doesn't want to admit it."

Cassie's gaze sharpened. "Is he cute? Hot? Smoking hot?"

I laughed. "I'm not really sure. He was buck naked when he took on human form and let's just say it was hard to keep my eyes on anything above the waist."

"Hot damn!" Cassie stood and came around her desk. "Go for it, girl. I don't know much about badger shifters, but if he's like all the others, you could totally hit that if you wanted to."

My thoughts shifted to the guy in the bar. *That's* what I wanted to hit.

"You sound like Sylvie," I complained. "And I don't want to hit that. Cassie, he was hung like a centaur."

"That's manageable with enough lube," she insisted, reminding me even more of Sylvie. "You haven't had a boyfriend in ages. Invite him to dinner next Sunday. If he's been up on that mountain for months, then he's probably dying for a good meal."

"From what I gather, his idea of a good meal is earthworms," I countered. What was it with my sisters lately? Actually, I knew what was up with them. They'd all found love and paired off, and now wanted me to do the same. Then they'd probably start pestering Babylon, if they weren't already.

"I'm making lasagna. Tell him to throw on some clothes and join us, then afterward the two of you can go get drinks at Pete's and get acquainted."

I sighed. "Knock it off, Cassie. He's not my type."

She leaned on the edge of her desk, fixing me with a perceptive look. "And what *is* your type?"

I thought once more of the man in the bar. Then I thought of my dreams, of a monster with horns and glowing eyes. What kind of weirdo was I? That had been a *dream*. If I encountered such a creature in real life chasing me through the woods, I wouldn't be turned on and dragging the guy into my bed or screwing him under the stars in a hay field.

But the dude in the bar? Let's just say I was hoping putt-putt ended up with *that* guy in my bed.

"I don't know how to define it," I confessed. "But I *do* know that I want to feel that spark of passion when I look at him, not wonder if he needs a shoe horn and a gallon of lube to get it in."

"Like Eddy, that guy you dated in college?"

Eddy. Nice, human Eddy. He was sweet. We hung out, watched television, studied, talked about how many cats someone should have before they got labeled a Crazy Cat Person. Spoiler: it's seven unless you live on a farm and they're working cats. Then it's a dozen. Don't argue, it's a scientific fact. And Eddy had agreed. In fact, Eddy had agreed with everything. We were so compatible that our friends expected us to get engaged before we got our diplomas. Instead we'd just drifted away after college.

I didn't want one of those relationships where we were fighting all the time, tossing dishes at each other and screaming so loud the neighbors called the cops. I just wanted someone who was a bit like me, but not exactly like me. I wanted to occasionally disagree. I wanted us to argue, then both work toward a mutually satisfactory resolution because our love was more important than whatever crap we were fighting over. Then I wanted us to have mind-blowing makeup sex.

Yeah. That.

"I just moved into a new house," I reminded my sister. "Give me some time to get settled in before you start berating me about being a withered-up spinster."

Cassie scrunched up her face. "That's not what I meant, Addy. I just want to see you happy."

"I *am* happy," I insisted. "I love my work and my new home. I'm going to a party this week with Babylon. I've got four squirrels and a vulture living with me."

I have a date tonight. But I didn't want to clue her in on that until I was sure that Ty was going to be more than just a fun evening.

"I don't think your vulture counts." She glared at the animal who'd insisted on coming into her office with me. "Okay, but if you're not dating anyone by Christmas then I'm going to fix you up with someone."

"Not the werebadger," I told her with a laugh. "Please not the werebadger."

She grinned. "Okay, not the werebadger. Get going. I've got work to do and I'm sure you have a house to delouse or something like that."

I stood. "Roaches. Then starlings who are pooping all over some dude's BMW. Then carpenter bees boring into the side of a woman's garage."

"Exciting." She waved me on. "I'll see you Sunday. Love you, Addy."

"Love you too, Cass," I told her as I herded my sidekick out the door. "Love you too."

* * *

THE REST of the day went easy, for once. The roaches were amenable to relocation. The starlings were easily convinced that a nearby shopping center was a better place to hang out, and the carpenter bees liked the nice rotted log I provided them far more than the woman's garage. I swung by the grocery store and picked up several fifty-pound bags of dog food as well as a dozen bones from the butcher and something labeled as "squirrel feast." Then as a treat I stopped by the bar where Babylon worked for a drink—well, a drink and to talk to her about my date tonight with Ty. I might be reluctant to talk to Cassie about a possible romance, but Lonnie and I had always been close, not only because we were the youngest sisters, but because our magic was a bit "out there" compared to the other witches in our family.

Drake and the squirrels had been pissed that they couldn't go inside. They were even more pissed that I locked them in the truck and hung one of Bronwyn's amulet wards on the antenna to keep them in. The human world was far less tolerant of animals in business establishments, and I couldn't exactly pass off a vulture and four squirrels as service animals.

"Here. Eat up." Babylon plopped a plate of jalapeno poppers in front of me along with a cold beer, then sat down. "What brings you in today? You look like you're dying to tell me something."

It was Monday and the place was empty aside from a guy over at the corner of the bar nursing a pint. I motioned for my sister to sit down and slid the poppers to the center of the table. We munched on them while we chatted, then I remembered the bone.

"Hey, I found this up on Savior Mountain this morning," I told her as I dug it out of my pants pocket. "A huge oak tree had come down. It had a split down the middle with some horrible stinky black oozy stuff in it, and this."

Babylon took the bone from me and turned it over in her fingers. "Why would this be in a tree?"

I shrugged. "I assumed maybe some animal was hiding their food in that crack in the trunk? Dogs bury bones. Squirrels hide food."

"But this is weird," she mused. "At first glance I'd assume it was a long bone from a small mammal, but it's not shaped right for that. It looks more like a finger bone."

A finger bone that big wouldn't have been a small mammal. "That's creepy," I told her.

She grinned. "*I'm* creepy, remember? Babylon, the necromancer witch? The witch who loves all things dead?" She stuck the bone in her pocket. "I'll check it out when I get a chance. I've got a spell or two that will tell me what it is, or who it is. Maybe there was a graveyard up on Savior Mountain at one time, and the fallen tree turned up a few bones."

She was probably right. There were graveyards in Accident, but some folk didn't like the idea of burying their dead in a designated spot. Some folk didn't like burying their dead at all.

I changed the subject to something less ghoulish, and told Cassie about my other adventures on the mountain this morning.

"I didn't know badgers had giant schlongs," she said.

"His balls were proportionate." I took a sip of my beer, thinking how nice it was to not be sitting in front of the television with my pajamas on tonight. Cassie was right. I needed friends and I did need a boyfriend. Or at the very least I needed to get laid.

"It's not like you haven't seen most of the shifters in Accident totally naked." She waved a popper at me for emphasis. "Remember Marcus at the Fourth of July party two years ago?"

I rolled my eyes. "Marcus gets naked at the drop of a hat.

And he screws everything he can get his hands on. I can't believe Cassie dated him."

"Screwable, but not datable—that's what I always said." Lonnie stuffed the popper into her mouth.

I'd never really thought of Marcus as screwable. The panther shifter had always been too smooth for my tastes. Once again, the image of a horned figure came unbidden to my mind. Damn, that had been one sexy dream.

"Speaking of dates..." I wiggled my eyebrows at her. "Guess who has one tonight? This witch right here, that's who."

Lonnie squealed. "Who? Where? Oh shit, tell me it's not with the werebadger."

I recoiled in mock horror. "There's not enough lube in the world for that guy, no matter what Cassie says. No, I'm going out with a guy I met at Pistol Pete's at lunch. He's new in town. Some kind of fae. He's Master of the Hunt or something, which means he's got *dogs*!"

Lonnie squealed. I squealed. A dog lover. It was a match made in heaven. Hopefully he liked vultures and squirrels as well.

"Tell me what he looks like." She leaned her elbows on the table and put her chin in her hands.

"Tall, but not freakishly so." I frowned for a second. "Taller than any fae I've ever known. He's probably around six-one or six-two."

"That *is* tall for a fae," Lonnie commented. "I don't think I've ever seen one over five-six."

I shrugged. We had our fair share of fairies, pixies, and brownies, but maybe only the short ones were coming to Accident.

"Maybe he's a troll and is using glamour," she teased.

I laughed. "If so, then I hope he keeps the glamour up." I'd never been attracted to trolls, and I doubted Ty was one anyway. The supernatural beings that called Accident home came there to be themselves. Why would a troll bother to put up a glamour in a place where no one would give them a second glance in their true form, in a town where centaurs and even dragons walked around with hooves and scales?

"So…tall, and…?" Lonnie prompted.

"Black hair," I mused, remembering the gorgeous guy. "Like, super dark. It's not really curly, but it's got a bit of a wave to it. He's tan, like Mediterranean or mixed-race skin tone tan." That was unusual for fae as well, although I did hear there were some elves who had dark complexions. "Dark eyes. He's got broad shoulders, and when I went in to kiss him, I realized he was really muscled. I think the guy works out, although if he's got a pack of hounds, I can imagine he'd need to be fit."

"You *kissed* him?" Babylon grinned. "You just met the guy, and ten seconds later you're kissing him? In the middle of Pistol Pete's? Girl, I think this is the one."

"On the *cheek*." I laughed. "But I had to step into him, and oh my! Let me tell you, it was the toughest thing I've ever done to walk away from that."

"Well, you've got a date tonight, so you can anticipate not walking away." Babylon nodded knowingly. "Gonna take him home?"

I'd been envisioning that all day. "I think it's a better option than driving all the way back to Accident, then hauling over the mountain before dawn in a 'drive of shame.'"

"Just be careful," Lonnie warned. "I know you can take care of yourself, and you've got a big-ass vulture that would scare the shit out of anyone—fae or not—but you don't really know this guy. Maybe you should call around and check into him."

"And have it get back to Cassie?"

My sister nodded. It would get back to Cassie, and if this

didn't work out, I'd be subject to a huge interrogation at Sunday dinner. And if it did work out, I'd be pestered to bring him to Sunday dinner. That might be moving a bit fast. Subjecting a new boyfriend of five days to my six sisters, their mates, and my cousin might send the guy screaming.

"I'll be careful," I promised Babylon.

What could go wrong? I was a grown woman, a witch, and I had a vulture and four squirrels in my house as well as a scary-looking dog-thing in my garage. If Ty turned out to be a weirdo or a total hose-bag, I'd just sic Yeth on him.

CHAPTER 10

ADRIENNE

"The harvest party is going to be fun," Babylon commented as she walked me out. "Bring Ty. I want to meet him, but I promise not to go all Cassie on you and grill the poor guy, or make things awkward."

I thought about that. If things worked out tonight, I definitely would invite Ty. Bonfire. Hot spiked cider. The smell of early autumn in the air. We could watch the sun go down, then sneak off to some dark corner to make out in the soft grass. Oh yeah.

There was only one problem with this party—five problems, actually.

"What am I going to do with Drake?" I mused. "And the squirrels?"

Babylon chuckled. "You know how in love I am with your vulture. He can come. In fact, let him ride shotgun and put Ty in the backseat. But squirrels? What's up with that, Addy?"

I looked over at my truck, noticing several pairs of eyes glaring at me from the back window. "I tried to evict them from someone's attic and they were a total pain. I had to cage them, and one bit me. When I went to release them in the woods they wouldn't go. Next thing I know they're inside my house, eating popcorn and watching a Hitchcock movie with me and Drake."

"How many squirrels?"

"Four." I dug my keys out of my bag, dreading what the inside of my truck probably looked like. "Three are pretty normal squirrel types, but the fourth is kinda weird. He's like their spokes-squirrel or something. I named him Hemorrhoid."

Lonnie had a minor coughing fit. "*What?*"

"Rhoid for short. The first day they were fine being left in the house while I worked, but today they insisted on coming with me. I had to lock them in the car with Drake just now and set a ward, otherwise they would have followed me in here."

She eyed the truck. "Well, bribe them. Convince them that if they're nice while you're gone, that you'll roast chestnuts or something."

I hugged Lonnie goodbye. When I got inside to my truck I discovered that the squirrels had not taken confinement lightly. They'd crapped all over the backseat and chewed up a good bit of the upholstery. I mentally calculated how much this was going to cost me to repair, then tried to scrape as much of the poop as I could out of the truck and onto the parking lot.

I drove home with the windows down, trying not to gag at the horrible smell. Worse, Drake wouldn't speak to me or even look at me. The vulture sat in the passenger seat sulking the entire way to our house, then hopped out and strode right through the front door and into my bedroom. I felt like a total shit, but I couldn't exactly take him into the bar and leave the squirrels behind. Actually I wasn't sure I could even take him into the bar. Babylon loved him, but the human who owned the joint might not want a giant bird in his establishment. Besides, I'd hoped he would prove a good influence on the squirrels or at least try to keep them from trashing my truck. Evidently I'd been wrong.

"Drake, I'm so sorry." I went into my bedroom while the squirrels dove into "Squirrel's Feast" which turned out to be an assortment of nuts and corn. "If it makes you feel any better, Babylon said you could come with me to the party this week."

The vulture huffed and turned his head away from me.

"I'll let you ride shotgun." I thought of Ty. "Although I might be taking a date with me, so maybe instead you can stay home and I'll take you somewhere special the next morning? I know, we'll go collect dead animals off the highway! How about that?"

He huffed, but tilted his head in a way that told me the idea appealed to him. Vultures. Collecting dead things off the highway always ranked higher than a bonfire party in their minds.

"Come on, buddy. If we lived in Accident then I could take you everywhere with me, but things aren't like that here. You must know that. You've been living out here your whole life and haven't been able to go into bars or sleep at the end of someone's bed. I try to take you everywhere I can, but there are going to be some places you're just not allowed."

Drake hissed and stomped his feet.

I reached over and put my arms around him. "I know things were different then. It was before you met me, before I met you. You're my best friend, Drake. But best friends don't go everywhere together. There will be times you can't be with me—like some human establishments, and times when I'm trying to get busy with a hot guy."

He leaned over and put his head against mine. *I under-stand the mating thing, but I need to be with you. We're bonded.*

We were. Best friends didn't fully describe our relationship. He was my familiar, and I was his witch. What we had was something special. I planted a kiss on top of his sharp beak and stroked his feathers.

"Forgive me?" He grunted and I smiled. "Good. How about a snack before I go on my date?"

A snack for Drake consisted of a piece of raw steak. I hand fed it to him, then raced to shower and change for my date. Before I headed out, I poured the dog food I'd bought earlier into a huge bowl and put it in the garage, making sure everything was welcome for Yeth. Then I went to the front porch to wait.

Ty pulled into my driveway right on time. He was in a sleek black BMW sedan that looked like it cost more than my house. I was used to the fact that supernaturals tended to accumulate wealth due to their longevity, and I knew how fae loved to be flashy, so I wasn't surprised in his choice of vehicle. I was surprised at how my heart sped up to see him swing out of the car wearing a long, black cashmere coat. I stood, and as he walked toward me I noticed he had on a dark grey suit with a white silk shirt that had the first few buttons undone. The effect was breathtaking.

Ty started up my porch, only to stop abruptly. Crap the wards. I quickly skipped down the steps and looped my arm in his, hoping he didn't see my magical security system as unwelcoming, or think me paranoid or anything.

He tucked my arm against his waist and turned, leading me to the car. "Good evening, Addy. You're looking lovely."

Jeans and a clean shirt weren't exactly my idea of lovely, and I was feeling a bit underdressed compared to him. Who the heck wears a suit to play putt-putt? Not that I was complaining, because the guy looked completely delicious.

"Hi." I cleared my throat, trying not to sound like a starstruck teenager. "Hi. Are you ready for some mini-golf action?"

"Is that what putt-putt is? Not that I totally understand the idea of mini golf either. Tiny golf clubs and pea-sized golf balls? Do we have to play the course on our knees?" His little sideways smile made me weak in the knees.

"It's eighteen holes of putting—which is why the putt-putt name. They've got obstacles and the courses have themes. It's kinda cheesy, but fun." I elbowed him playfully as we walked to the car.

"What does the winner get?" He hesitated before opening my door.

"Well, if you sink the last shot with a hole-in-one, then you get a free soda. We keep score, but that's just for fun, unless you'd like to suggest a friendly wager, that is."

He opened the door, his arm easing out from under mine as he placed a hand on my back. "I'm always open for a wager. Winner gets…?"

The heat of his hand seared me clear through my coat. I slid into the seat and debated whether I should suggest that the loser bought hot dogs and soda, or whether the winner got oral sex. I knew which one I wanted the most, but I'd just met Ty and didn't want to commit myself to giving a blow job just yet.

"A kiss."

"Just a kiss?" He held the door open, his smile so damned sexy.

"Just a kiss." I took a deep breath and slowly let it out. "For now. I reserve the right to change my mind later."

He laughed, a deep throaty sound that shot heat down right between my legs. Then he closed the door and walked around to climb in the driver's side.

The drive to the putt-putt course was only about twenty minutes. He asked me about my day and I went into great detail as tales of insect infestations, rats, and naked badgers made him laugh. I loved the sound of his laugh. By the time we pulled into the parking lot of the mini golf course, I was ready to suggest we head to a hotel.

But instead I tried to compose my raging libido while he walked around to open the door for me.

Hole In One mini-golf was a go-to entertainment venue for the folks in Accident. It was outside the wards, so the owner's customer base was more human than not, but the fact that the owner was a shark shifter meant he was open to shutting the park down for "private parties" where gnomes, or minotaurs, or pixies could party without fear of encountering humans. The place had originally been owned by a human husband and wife team who'd sold it to Antwan and retired to Florida five years ago. It was off one of those rural routes that was just far enough out of town to be somewhat isolated, but near enough that it was easy to pop over for a game. Antwan had planted a few dense rows of evergreens outside of a tall stockade fence so looking into the course from outside was pretty close to impossible for anyone without wings or some super leaping skills. It kept the curious humans out when folks with wings and horns were playing.

Today the course was open to the public and we weren't the only couple who were here at seven o'clock on a Monday night. A group of six teenagers were sipping sodas and arguing over who was going to get which color ball. An elderly couple were already on the course, carefully planning each stroke. Two men were arguing over their scorecards and calling each other duffers.

Ty walked up to the counter and blinked in surprise when he saw Antwan. I giggled, knowing everyone had the same reaction when they first saw the sharkshifter. He was built like he should be a bouncer outside a rowdy club, with shoulders so wide I sometimes wondered how he got through a doorway, and a bald head that gleamed a warm brown in the artificial light of the course.

"Two?" Antwan glanced over at me and smiled. "Addy! Nice to see ya girl. How's the rat-and-bat business going?"

"It's keeping me in meat and potatoes." I reached out and put my hand on Ty's arm. To Antwan's credit, he didn't even raise an eyebrow.

"Well, game's free for my favorite witch." His grin stiffened a little as he glanced over at Ty, and the implication was clear. Mess with my friend, and you'll know what it feels like to have a Great White bite your leg clean off.

I rolled my eyes and grabbed my club.

"His favorite witch?" Ty and I walked over to where the colored golf balls were. He didn't sound jealous, or the least bit worried about the nonverbal threat he'd just been handed. I liked that. Jealousy was such a pain in the ass to deal with, and I wasn't one of those girls who was turned on by two guys duking it out either.

"We're all his favorite witches," I told Ty. "All seven of us."

He picked up a bright yellow ball and handed it to me. Had he known this was my favorite color, or was this just a lucky guess? As I took it from him, my fingers brushed his and I caught my breath.

"Seven? Your coven?" He picked up the red ball and it took me a second to realize what he meant.

"Oh no, my sisters. We're all witches. I'm the second youngest." I wasn't sure if his type of fae had family units or not, and it seemed a bit rude to ask, so instead I shot him a cocky grin and strolled over to the first hole, placing my yellow ball on the X. "Get ready to lose, hound-boy. I've been honing my skills at mini golf since I was five, and I'm gonna beat the pants off you."

"That's what I'm hoping," he teased.

I tapped the ball and watched as it rolled up and down the fake green hills, weaving back and forth until it bounced off the backstop and into the hole.

"Booya!" I put my hands in the air. "Beat that one, buddy."

He didn't but came close, sinking the red ball in two strokes. We spent the next hour smack-talking, and flirting. Ty resorted to trying to distract me by running his hands down my waist to my hips, or whispering naughty things in my ear. It worked, but in the end I still won the match.

"Winner gets a kiss," he whispered before turning me around and dipping his head.

His lips met mine, soft, warm, and gentle. Time seemed to stand still, then I moved into him and wrapped my arms around his neck. His tongue touched the seam of my mouth, asking even though I could feel from the tension in his body that he was fighting to hold himself back. I opened for him, and everything caught fire. His tongue licked mine and we pressed together, practically devouring each other on the eighteenth hole of the putt-putt course.

When we finally came up for air, I was breathless, hot, and desperate to have him naked and inside me.

"Let's get out of here," I whispered, well aware that a few of the other patrons were beginning to look our way. Normally I wouldn't mind, but having an audience of six teens wasn't my thing.

"And go where?" He turned me in his arms so my back was against his front, then nibbled down the side of my neck as he pressed my ass against that rock-hard erection.

I didn't have the patience for driving all over town looking for a hotel, and I certainly didn't have the patience for the thirty-minute drive into Accident. That left one choice.

"My place."

He stilled, and for a second I thought something might be wrong.

"Are you sure?"

"Yes, I'm sure." Was he just being gentlemanly? Like the opening door thing? Or was I detecting a note of regret in his voice?

Before I could think further, he spun me around and kissed me again, driving every last bit of doubt from my mind.

The ride back to my place seemed excruciatingly long. He opened the car door for me and I fell into his arms. For a moment, I wondered if we'd even make it into the house, or end up doing it here on my lawn, but he pulled away with ragged breathing and yanked me toward the door. I barely had time to dismiss the wards and unlock the deadbolt before I was in his arms again.

Buttons popped and clothes tore. He pushed me back against the wall, knocking over a lamp and two picture frames along the way. I frantically tried to kick off the remains of my pants and my underwear as his hands grabbed my ass and hoisted me up. My legs wrapped around his hips and I gasped as he eased himself inside.

Damn, he felt good. I wanted to take my time, but I was hungry and desperate. Round two would be more leisurely. Right now I wanted hard and fast.

One of his hands held my butt while the other gripped my hair. His mouth left mine and he buried his face into my neck with a sexy growl, nipping the skin gently. I tilted my head back, encouraging him with breathless moans. My nails dug into his shoulders and I felt my orgasm swell, then crest. I shook in his arms as he came. We stood against the wall for a few ragged breaths, then he dropped down onto the couch, pulling me on top of him. His hands caressed down my back and I rested my cheek on his chest thinking that this was the best sex I'd ever had—better even than those dreams the past few nights.

And if this fast-hard-quickie had been good, imagine how incredible it would be once we took our time and explored at our leisure.

Holy feathers and fur, it had been amazing. I mean A-maze-ing. My whole body tingled and all I could think of was doing it again, and again, and again. Could I reschedule my appointments for tomorrow and just have sex with Ty all day long? I'm pretty sure a fae didn't have anything pressing to do. Well, except feed his hounds, and maybe he could call a neighbor in Accident to do that for him.

This guy…he was funny, smart, courteous. He was gorgeous, built like a freaking god, and the sex had been damned mind-blowing.

I sat up, straddling him. "Do you want to go to a bonfire tomorrow night?" I asked, thinking an invitation to my family Sunday night dinner wouldn't be super appropriate yet.

He stretched, then pulled me back down against his chest. "I'd love to."

Actually I was hoping he'd spend the night and I'd see him first thing in the morning.

"Maybe I can stay, and we can do breakfast?" he asked, as if reading my mind.

"I'd like that." I planted a quick kiss on his shoulder and got up, pushing away his hands as he tried to pull me back down. "I'll be right back."

I had to use the bathroom, then maybe I'd fix us something to eat. Or maybe I'd just sprawl over top of him again and go for round two. With a quick smile over my shoulder at the sexy man on my couch, I snuck into the bedroom and into the adjoining bathroom, ignoring the questioning glance from Drake and the squirrels.

As I was freshening up, I heard them all heading into the living room and winced. I wondered if Ty liked birds and squirrels as much as he liked dogs? Suddenly the living room erupted in sound. I heard Ty shout, then Drake started shrieking and hissing. The squirrels made their "danger" noises. Rhoid screamed. I ran out of the bathroom still naked and into the living room to see an equally naked Ty throttling one of my squirrels.

"Don't you run away, you bastard," he snarled. "You won't escape me. I'm going to pop your head right off and drag you back where you belong."

"No!" I shouted, horrified by the situation. When had the suave sexy guy I was half in love with turned into some kind of monster who hurts poor defenseless squirrels?

Ty froze, Rhoid dangling from his hands. The squirrel bit down hard on his finger. He yelped but held on.

"Drop the squirrel," I commanded.

Sorrow flickered across his face, then his expression hardened. "No. I can't. I'm sorry, but I have to take him with me."

What the hell was going on? We'd had a wonderful date. We'd had sex. And now he was throwing that all away to kill a squirrel?

"I'm sorry," he repeated. "I promise the makeup sex will be really good. I'll even grovel a little. I just have to kill him and take him to hell first."

Oh, there would be no makeup sex, even if he groveled on hands and knees. I wasn't going to be having sex with anyone who murdered squirrels.

I set my jaw and tried to look intimidating, even though I was naked. "I *said*, drop the squirrel. You drop that squirrel right now and get out of my house or I'll...I'll... You'll regret it."

I was bluffing. This was me, a vulture, and the three

squirrels that weren't in Ty's grip against a powerful supernatural being. Correction, me and a vulture. The other squirrels had vanished into the basement, and I sensed them hiding in the furnace room. Reaching out my awareness, I realized it *was* just me and Drake. Sucked, because I could really use Yeth right now.

Ty's eyes glowed red and horns sprouted from his head. He was still a breathtakingly handsome guy, but his resemblance to the demon from my dreams was startling.

Shit. Double shit. If seeing him throttling my squirrel wasn't enough of a punch in the gut, this throwback to my erotic dreams was doubly so. What the hell was going on? Why had the…whatever of my dreams become someone who could hurt a harmless woodland creature?

"Ty, what is going on?" I pleaded, changing tactics. "That squirrel is under my protection. Why are you harming him? Why would you hurt someone I care for?"

Unreadable emotions flickered across his face, then he took a breath and stood straight, gripping Rhoid tightly. "You don't understand. This has nothing to do with you. He's ours. He belongs to me."

"No, he's mine," I snapped. "Put down the squirrel and get out. Out! I want you out of my house. I never want to see you again, ever!"

He stared at me, stunned. "But the makeup sex…"

I stomped my foot. "No makeup sex. No sex ever again. Let go of my squirrel and get out."

Suddenly my living room was filled with dog-things. There were a dozen of them—one headed, two headed, all with sharp white teeth and glowing eyes. I recognized three from my lawn last night—and I recognized Yeth. He cringed, not meeting my gaze.

I felt dizzy. Yeth. Hounds. Master of the Hounds. Ty, or whoever he was, had sent his hounds to watch me days ago.

Had the meeting at Pistol Pete's been planned? Our date? Sex? All to get a *squirrel*? Anger filled me along with sorrow, and embarrassment.

"You bastard!" I spat at Ty. "You asshole!"

He recoiled, and his grip on Rhoid must have loosened because the squirrel squirmed free and dashed for me.

"No! Damnit, get back here," he shouted.

The dog-things charged. I couldn't believe this was happening. The first guy I fall for since college and he was only using me for his ulterior hellish motive. And now he was siccing his hounds on me, willing them to maul me. I'd had sex with this guy. I'd opened myself up to this guy. The betrayal cut deep.

Cassie was the sister known for her hot temper, but rage flared through normally placid me—rage and hurt.

"Sit!" I yelled with every bit of authority I possessed as I let my magic fly. I swore I'd never do this, but I was *so* angry.

The hellhounds sat as if their back legs had been rendered instantly useless. They snarled, scooting forward with their front legs like dogs dragging their asses across the carpet.

"Down! Stay!"

That did it. The hounds dropped to the ground, immobile. My stomach churned and I felt nauseated as the magic rolled through me—nauseated as well by the thought of what I'd done. I'd seized control of their physical forms. I'd made them my puppets. They might still be snarling, but they were unable to move.

That should have been enough but I was still caught up in a storm of anger. There he was, standing there with his tousled black hair and his chiseled cheekbones, and his kissable lips and dark sultry eyes. How dare he be so damned sexy. How dare he do this to me.

"Nice puppies!" I shouted.

The magic reached a crescendo, and I nearly barfed. It hit

the hellhounds full force, pouring out of me and leaving me drained and shaken. The hounds stopped snarling. Happy tongues lolled out of mouths and tails began to wag furiously. I'd taken control of their bodies, and now I'd just taken control of their minds.

"What have you done?" Ty looked at his pack, then glared over at me. "I'm Master of the Hellhounds. What have you done to them?"

I glared right back. "You might be Master of the Hellhounds when you're in hell, but this is *my* home. I'm not going to stand by and let your animals chew me to pieces."

"I'm not...they weren't..." His eyes narrowed and his gaze shifted to the squirrel on my shoulder. "Give him to me. Give me that sneaky little bastard."

That's what this was about? He wanted Rhoid for some reason? He seduced me as part of a ploy to get a *squirrel*? If he'd hit me up with this request a few days ago and asked nicely, I might have handed over all four of them, but the pesky animals had become part of my little family and the only way they were leaving my home was if they did it of their own volition.

"Get your own squirrel. This one's mine." Wait, what did he want a squirrel for? Now I was thinking of all the nefarious things the jerk might want to do to a poor furry thing. Was he going to use it as bait in some hellhound fight? Turn it into a hellsquirrel? That last one might actually be kind of cool, but I was totally against the first. Hunting was a way of life for many in Accident, and I wasn't averse to chowing down on a good steak, but taking a life for sustenance was different than a poor animal being sacrificed to a bunch of hellhounds.

"He's *mine*, not yours," Ty snapped. "I had him first. He escaped and I've been looking for him for centuries."

I rolled my eyes. Such drama. There's no way he'd been

looking for a lost squirrel for *centuries*. The guy was a jerk and a liar.

"Well, finders keepers, losers weepers. You've got yourself a dozen dog-things, you don't need this squirrel, especially if you've lived just fine without it for *centuries*. What do you want with him anyway?"

"He's mine for all of eternity. I have to torture him, and I'm way behind on his punishment," Ty shouted.

Oh, he was so not getting this squirrel—or any squirrel for that matter. In fact, I might not even let him take the hell-hounds back with him. Did he torture them as well? Poor puppers, no wonder they were so on edge. They just needed some love, a nice comfy pillow, and a whole lot of liver treats and they'd be fine. I'd bet I could quickly find nice families to adopt them.

"If anyone is going to be punishing anybody, it's me," I shouted back. Hearing an alarmed squeak I turned to Rhoid. "Don't worry. I'm not talking about you, I'm talking about him. Ooo, just wait until I get my hands on him."

Sadly that statement was followed by all sorts of lurid fantasies that had very little to do with punishment. Damn him for being so sexy! And what was with me still wanting this guy after he'd shown himself to be a total douche-canoe?

Ty threw his hands up in the air, then took a step toward me. "Addy listen, you're being completely irrational here. Just give me the squirrel. If I don't take him, someone else will— and they might not be as nice about it."

My entire body tingled at the way he said my name, and now I was mad again. "*I'm* being irrational? You pretend to like me, then the moment I invite you into my house you have sex with me, then bring out your attack hounds and try to steal my squirrel. Go back to hell. Go, and don't come back. And leave these sweet puppies. You don't deserve them."

He ground his teeth. "Addy, he's not a squirrel, he's a soul that escaped from hell. And I didn't tell my hounds to attack you. I'd never let them do that. They're here to grab the squirrel, Faust. They were going to secure him and bring him to hell."

There he was, that sexy guy again, but I couldn't forget coming out of my bedroom to find him strangling a squirrel, even if he was telling the truth and Rhoid *was* a soul that had escaped from hell. And I couldn't forgive the fact that he'd set this all up just to get a soul back.

He didn't really like me. He didn't really want me. Yeah, he'd obviously enjoyed sex with me, but it was all done with an ulterior motive. I didn't matter to him.

It made me want to cry, and I'd be damned if I cried in front of this asshole.

"Get out." For a brief second I thought about turning his hounds on him, but I'd already crossed the line with them and done something I swore I'd never do. I wouldn't make it worse by forcing them to attack their own master.

Ty looked at me, then at the squirrel, then back at me. "Okay. I'm sorry, Addy."

He wasn't sorry. He wasn't sorry at all. Picking up the nearest thing at hand, which happened to be a scented candle, I threw it at him. "Get. Out."

He vanished, leaving an expensive BMW in my driveway, a dozen hounds on my living room floor, and me with tears stinging my eyes. Without another word, I left everyone behind, went into my bedroom, closed the door and cried.

CHAPTER 11

TYPHON

I'd fucked up big time. I'd had Faust in my hands and I'd let him go. It was my duty. I was in charge of his torture when he'd escaped, and it was my duty to bring him back to hell. What sort of demon was I to let a soul slip through my fingers a second time?

But the hurt and betrayal in Addy's eyes had been more than I could bear. If I'd pushed her aside and grabbed Faust, if I'd hauled him off to hell, she would have never forgiven me. I wasn't sure she'd forgive me now. How could I explain to her that the squirrel in her house wasn't a squirrel, that he was a magic-using soul who'd escaped hell and was hiding behind her for protection?

There was a reason Faust had gone to hell. He'd bargained his soul away, and after centuries of squirming through loopholes, it had been time for him to pay the piper. But even after death, he'd wiggled free of his obligations. And tonight I'd let him go because I didn't want a witch to think I was harming a helpless animal.

How could she believe I'd ever set my hounds on her? That I or anything obedient to me would ever harm her?

When I'd felt her magic take their will, I'd let them go. I didn't want to fight her for the obedience of my hounds. As mortifying as it was to return to hell without them, I'd far rather do that then rip them free of her. That would only harm them, harm her, and harm me.

"Give her solace," I whispered through the link I shared with my hounds. "Comfort her in my stead." I made them stay, freed them to obey her even without her magic. Yeth was already half in love with her, the dog, but the others hadn't been exposed to her enough to be seduced by the more subtle notes of her magic.

But *was* it magic? I thought about the evening we'd spent playing putt-putt, how we'd laughed and flirted. I enjoyed her company. Being with her was more fun than tossing murderers into pits of hellfire. It wasn't just sex. I *liked* her.

And yeah, the sex. That had been pretty damned amazing as well.

"Did you retrieve your lost soul, Hound Master?" Abraxas slid up beside me, eyeing the soul of a murderer that I'd been ignoring while I thought about Addy.

"Not yet."

"Now that he's been located, Satan himself as well as the prince have asked me to assist."

The asshole sounded completely smug about this. "I'll handle it. Go back to the fourth circle and…do whatever you need to do there. I've got Faust."

"Like you had him centuries ago?" Abraxas shot his long, forked tongue out between his lips and smacked the murderer in the face. The man screamed, the demon's tongue leaving a smoldering red mark on his cheek.

"Fuck off, Abraxas." I scowled. "My hounds and I have done all the work these centuries to find Faust. We've found him, and I'm the one that will bring him in."

The other demon shrugged. "The boss himself told me to assist. If you don't need my help though…"

I glared at Abraxas. "I don't need your help."

The saccharine smile he gave me was anything but reassuring. "Fine then, Typhon. Happy hunting."

He walked away, and something sour curdled in my stomach. Abraxas wasn't going to let this one be. He wanted the glory, the acclaim for bringing in Faust. He wanted to be promoted above me, to perhaps become Master of the Hounds in my place. That wasn't going to happen.

And his involvement put me in a very awkward position. I needed to bring Faust in myself. But I also needed to make things right with Addy because there was no way I'd hurt her again. I needed her. I wanted her. And although she might never want to see me again, I wouldn't risk her hating me just to bring in a soul I'd let slip through my hands centuries ago.

CHAPTER 12

ADRIENNE

The *nerve* of that man. Or demon. Whatever. I'd cried my eyes out, then came out of my bedroom to find an entire menagerie in my house. The squirrels had barricaded themselves in the kitchen and were chattering angrily at the hellhounds lazing around my living room floor. Drake played referee over the whole lot of them, perched on the coffee table and swiveling his head to eye each group with scorn.

I plopped down on the sofa and teared up again, struggling not to cry in front of his hellhounds, even though they'd stayed behind with me. Not that they'd chosen to. I'd commanded them, forced their wills to mine. I'd swore I'd never do such a thing, but I had. In anger.

But did I have any choice? If I hadn't turned his hellhounds to my side, he would have taken that squirrel and done who knows what with the poor thing.

Drake nudged my shoulder with his beak, and I turned to bury my face in his musty smelling feathers.

"He was just using me," I muttered into the bird. "Using me to get the squirrel."

He cares about you, Yeth told me. *He was not lying when he said we were not to hurt you. Ever since he met you in that bar, he has been under your thrall. Actually, he was under your thrall since he first entered your dream and you cast your witchy spell upon him.*

Entered my dream? Holy shit on toast, had Ty actually been the sexy horned demon from my dream the other night? Even though that ratcheted up my libido quite a bit, it also made me even more pissed at him. Why the fuck had he entered my dream? Had he been plotting this since before I met him in Pistol Pete's? Was this all a ruse to get the squirrel? Did I mean nothing to him at all?

As for him being enthralled by me…pffft. That was total bullshit. I'd never cast a spell over him. I'd done nothing but be myself. How dare he pull this "she enthralled me" crap, when he was the one catfishing me to get to a squirrel that was living in my house.

Drake hissed at the hellhound, then told me I should talk to the squirrel I'd named Hemorrhoid. I sniffed, thinking over what had happened from a less emotional perspective. Ty had claimed that Rhoid was an escaped soul, that he was someone named Faust.

I frowned, remembering my college literature classes. Was this the Faust who'd made a deal with the devil? If so, then his soul was destined for hell. But why was he a squirrel in my house? How had a fifteenth-century man who'd bargained his soul for riches and knowledge ended up a squirrel I'd evicted from a woman's house?

How the mighty had fallen.

I pulled away from Drake and sniffed, wiping my eyes. The hounds were still chilling in front of me. The squirrels were still in the kitchen, anxious and restless. I closed my eyes and thought for a moment, then decided I needed to put my emotions and libido aside and get to the bottom of this whole thing.

"Hounds." I stood and faced the lazy canines. "You all will sleep in my garage tonight. I release you. You are free to stay, sleep, and eat what I provide, or you may return to your infernal home and master. It's your choice, but you cannot stay inside my house tonight."

They stood and stretched, grumbling a bit at being denied a cozy night in my living room. I grabbed the bag of dog food I'd bought earlier, and they perked up, following me into the garage. I poured food into several bowls and dishes, then added a few blankets and pillows and several buckets of fresh water. Leaving the garage door open enough for them to go as they pleased, I wished them good night, then went back inside, sealing the wards around the garage. I trusted the hounds since I'd bound them to me, but I wanted to give them the freedom to leave if they chose, but not open my house up to whatever monsters might want to enter—including Ty.

"You," I pointed at Rhoid. "I need to talk to you."

The other three squirrels took off and hid under the couch. Rhoid looked as if he were about to do the same.

"I protected you. I stood here in my living room and faced down a demon and a pack of hellhounds to keep you from being dragged off to hell. The very least you owe me is an explanation."

Rhoid squeaked and patted a little paw on his chest, an innocent-squirrel look on his face.

"Talk, or I'll kick you outside of my house and outside of the wards," I told him. "My magic is wearing off the hellhounds. They'll hunt you down and have you within minutes without my protection."

Rhoid sighed then hopped along the edge of the counter,

leaping ten feet onto the nearest chair where he sat with his arms crossed in front of him.

"Are you really Faust? *The* Faust?" I waited for his nod. "Tell me how you ended up in hell, how you managed to escape, and everything since then."

I made a bargain with Satan when I was alive, he told me. *Through smarts, trickery, and magic I managed to live for nearly three hundred years, but Satan finally outwitted me and I died, my soul forfeit to hell for all eternity.*

I had no idea what his original bargain had been, but he'd gone into it with open eyes and managed to evade paying the price for far longer than had been the original intent of the deal. As much as the idea of hell's punishments gave me the creeps, the guy had willingly entered into this deal.

After suffering for a few decades, I bribed and tricked a few demons, then stole Charon's boat and managed to escape. But one of the demons I'd tricked was smarter than I thought and my resurrection spell came with a curse.

You're a squirrel. That's your curse.

He nodded. *Do you know how sick I am of eating nuts and cracked corn? Of having sex with squirrels? I can't even perform magic like this.* He held up his tiny paws. *Ever since I escaped hell I've been like this, trying somehow to break the curse.*

"Well, I can't help you break the curse. That's not the sort of magic I can do," I told him. What I didn't tell him was that one of my sisters might be able to help him. Sylvie was a luck witch, and also had the opposite skill. If she couldn't break a curse, then I was pretty sure Cassie could. But I wasn't offering that up at this point. I might never offer that up. Being a squirrel was a better fate than being tortured in hell, and I couldn't justify Rhoid avoiding all that he'd agreed to when he'd sold his soul to Satan. Plus he *was* a bit of a jerk. There was a reason I'd named him Hemorrhoid, after all.

I didn't come with you because I thought you could break the curse, although that would have been an added benefit, Rhoid said. *I came with you because I knew you could protect me against Typhon and his hounds. I saw the effect you had on my squirrel friends, and knew you had the power to wrest control of the hellhounds away from their demon master. And I saw what a soft, weak, emotional response you had toward animals. I knew you'd protect me.*

I was starting to regret that I had protected him. Rhoid had used me just as Typhon had used me. Both of them deserved to be tossed out of my house and left to their own fates. But if I'd escaped hell as a squirrel with a pack of hellhounds and demons after me, maybe I'd use a capable witch for my protection as well. I couldn't completely blame Rhoid, even though he *was* a total asshole.

And I couldn't completely blame Ty either. Faust had made a deal then welched on it. Ty was just doing his job in trying to retrieve him. And if I'd had a job to do and encountered a warded house with my quarry locked inside, I might try to sneak in via a dream as well.

It wasn't Ty's fault the dream had turned erotic. That… that was probably on both of us. There was an attraction there, and I knew it wasn't just on my side. Yeth had said Ty had thought himself enchanted. Maybe he'd doubted our attraction to each other just as I'd doubted his intentions.

Yes, he wanted Faust back, but now that I thought about it, he truly hadn't tried to attack me with his hellhounds. Plus if he'd wanted inside my house to get the squirrel, he wouldn't have had to endure a putt-putt date with me when he could have broken through the wards and forced his way in.

And he'd left when I told him to, although I knew if he really wanted he could have overpowered me, even with his hellhounds as happy puppies. My magic worked on them, but not on him, and he was far stronger than I was. I had no real defense against demon magic. But he'd walked away from Faust, a soul he'd been hunting down for centuries, because I'd told him to.

Maybe there was some sort of compromise we could reach where Faust paid per the terms of his contract, but not necessarily the traditional hellish punishments. I needed to think on it before I reached out to contact Ty, though. And I definitely needed to get my emotions and heart under control before I saw him again.

You're not going to turn me over to him, are you? Rhoid asked, twisting his paws nervously together.

"I don't know. You made a deal, and it's not my place to protect you when you refuse to hold up your end of the bargain." Ugh. This was going to get ugly if I couldn't come up with some compromise. If Ty went to Lucien and complained that I was protecting Faust, things would get very prickly in my family. I wasn't even sure Cassie would stick up for me on this one. Rhoid *had* sold his soul after all.

Unless there was a weird loophole in the contract. I wasn't a lawyer, but Cassie was. Maybe she could figure something out. It would be better than me trying to come up with a deal. The only problem with that was that I'd need to tell Cassie everything, and I wasn't sure I was ready to do that.

But there was one of my sisters I'd definitely tell. Tomorrow. After a good night's sleep, that is.

"Go hide under the couch with your buddies," I told Rhoid. "I promise I won't do anything tonight."

CHAPTER 13

ADRIENNE

"You don't have a lot of choices here, Addy," Babylon wiped the bar down, then started washing glasses while I munched on a sandwich. "Turn the squirrel over, go to Cassie and Lucien and see if they can modify the contract somehow, or spend the rest of your life with this Faust barricaded inside your house."

I really didn't like the last idea, and it wouldn't work anyway. "He won't stay behind. He insists on coming everywhere with me now. I'm literally going on calls with a vulture and four squirrels crammed into the cab of my truck."

Lonnie winced. "Honestly I'd just turn the damned thing over to the demon and wash my hands of the whole thing."

I groaned. "If he was in human form I'd totally do it, but he's this cute, adorable, fuzzy squirrel. With little tiny paws, and a little twitchy nose, and big dark eyes."

"Yeah, they're just as cute when they're skeletons." Babylon sighed. "I get it. I really do."

"When I walked in and saw Ty holding that fuzzy little

guy up in the air like he was strangling him, I just lost it," I told her.

Lonnie nodded. "It would have been a different case if Ty were holding up a wizened old wizard who'd sold his soul centuries ago."

"I'm not sure I could have just excused Ty for choking an old man either." I picked at my French fries. "I'm going to have to go to Cassie. Which sucks. It's going to put her right in the middle between me and Lucien. I hate to do that."

"Eventually his job and ours was going to conflict," Lonnie pointed out. "Cassie will work it out. She always does. And the best part is that takes everything right out of your hands. No longer your responsibility."

Except Rhoid still would kind of be my responsibility. And I still didn't know what to do about Ty. Was there any way to make up with him after all that happened last night? Did I even want to make up with him?

"You're still coming to the party tonight, aren't you?" Lonnie asked.

I wrinkled my nose. "I probably shouldn't. I've got so much to do, and Rhoid won't stay home. It's probably not safe for him to be running around a corn maze and bonfire with half of hell after him."

Although I hadn't seen any of the hellhounds since last night. Neither had I seen Ty or any demons. Did Ty call a temporary truce? Were they waiting for an opportunity to jump on the squirrel and haul him back to hell?

"That's not your problem. If asshole Faust wants to leave your nice, safe, warded house, then that's on him." Babylon dried her hands and leaned over the bar. "Addy, you *are* coming to this party. You need to live your life. At no time did you promise to protect this squirrel who made the deci-sion to run and hide behind your skirts. He's the one who got himself in trouble. You've helped him far beyond what any witch would be expected to do."

"I don't know. I'd feel terrible if I was partying it up and demons trashed my house and took Rhoid to hell. Or if he got snatched out of my truck or the field while I was eating barbeque and drinking beer."

"What's the worst thing that could happen? Well, besides your house being trashed, that is. Faust already died once. So he dies again and spends a few days getting smacked around in hell until you pull enough strings to get him out on bail or get his sentence lessened. Thousands of people sell their souls to Satan, and they don't get the luxury of a few hundred extra years of life, then a few hundred more running around as a squirrel. Stop taking on the world's burdens, Addy. And especially stop taking on some asshole wizard's burdens."

She was right. "Okay. You win. I'm going to the party tonight. But first I'm dropping all these animals off at my house and forcing them to stay there while I go talk to Cassie."

And I did just that, although one animal I couldn't force to stay in my house. Drake came with me to the law firm where Cassie worked, waddling after me through the hallways and up the elevator to my sister's office. I'd called ahead of time to make sure Cassie put me in her schedule, and to let her know that I needed Lucien to be there as well.

My sister stood and came around the desk to give me a hug. Lucien stood beside her desk, a grim expression on his face. To his left stood another demon—one that I'd gotten to know carnally just last night.

Ty was sexy as hell in a black business suit, his dark hair brushed back from his forehead. Unlike Lucien, he didn't appear upset or angry. His expression was carefully blank, but as my eyes met his, I saw a brief flash of worry crease his forehead.

"Why are you sheltering this criminal?" Lucien snarled. "Nothing concerning Faust is your business."

"It became my business when a squirrel took shelter in my house," I snapped back. "I didn't know the details of his contract with your father, or even that he was a human. I let some squirrels live in my house, then suddenly last night a demon and a pack of hellhounds are trying to kill an animal I had under my protection in my own house."

"And now you know differently, so hand him over."

I folded my arms across my chest. "Nope. Not happening."

"Let's go over the contract Faust and your father's representative signed." Cassie moved back behind her desk and picked up a stack of papers. "Everybody sit while I read this."

"It's airtight," Lucien insisted. "His soul is ours. Our best contract lawyers in hell have looked at it."

"Well, *I* haven't and since Faust is here and not in hell, he's under our jurisdiction."

"He's not in Accident," Lucien argued. "You don't have any more standing outside of Accident than I do."

"No, but as the soul in question has claimed sanctuary in my sister's house, I *do* have jurisdiction. Our homes and places of business outside of Accident are still considered ours, just like embassies."

Lucien began to pace. I'd never seen him face off against my sister like this. He'd always seemed absolutely whipped, but maybe in private he actually stood up to her occasionally.

Nah.

Cassie flipped through the first two pages, then rubbed her forehead. "I don't know, Addy, this looks pretty solid. Can't you just give the guy back? He got way more than he'd bargained for in this contract from what I can see. It's time for him to pay the piper."

"Keep reading," I insisted. There had to be something I could do. There was no way I could look that squirrel in the eyes and send him off to hell for eternal torture.

"Addy, please," Ty pleaded. "His soul was legally bartered to us, and he's been evading his end of the bargain for far too long. There is no reason for you to give him sanctuary."

"Don't call me Addy, you asshole. Rather than come knock on my door when you realized I had Faust, you invade my dreams and have sex with me, then stalk me, ask me out on a date, and have sex with me again. Then once you're in my house and we're naked, you grab my squirrel and choke him."

"Wait…what?" Cassie pushed aside the stack of papers and stood. Fire crackled along her fingers as she glared at Ty.

"Dude, seriously?" Lucien shook his head at Ty, then eyed Cassie nervously. "You actually thought screwing a witch was a good way to grab a soul she was safeguarding?"

"She enchanted me, seduced me," Ty complained. "All I was trying to do was find a way to get inside her wards."

"More like find a way inside something else," I snapped.

"Oh, like I could help it. I can't resist you. The moment I'm with you I completely forget about my job, my hounds, the soul I've been trying to hunt down for centuries. If that damned squirrel hadn't come into the living room and broken your spell, I would have spent the night with you in absolute bliss."

Somehow that was equally flattering and maddening. "There is no spell, you moron. I haven't enchanted you. It's *you* who seduced *me*, who took advantage of me to get Faust."

"You slept with my sister?" Cassie's voice rose into a shriek. "Three times?"

Ty squirmed. "Twice was in her dreams, so that doesn't really count."

"Like hell it doesn't buster." I walked over and poked my finger into his chest.

"I don't like the idea of your demons screwing around with my family," Cassie snarled at Lucien.

"Well, it's a little late for that since four of your seven sisters are shacked up with various denizens of hell, not including you," Lucien snarled back.

"There's a difference between honest attraction and someone not being truthful about who he is and why he's seducing my sister in her dreams." Cassie jammed her hands on her hips.

I did the same. "Yeah. I didn't know you were the demon from my dreams when I met you at Pistol Pete's. I didn't suspect it until you sprouted horns as you were trying to strangle my squirrel. I didn't even realize you were a demon —I thought maybe you were fae."

"Fae!" Ty nearly spat as he said the word. "How could you ever think I was fae? How?"

Lucien stepped between us. "None of this matters. What *does* matter is that there is a soul we need to collect—a soul that legally belongs to us. Right, Cassie?"

My sister grumbled something about how someone was definitely not getting any sex tonight, then sat back down at her desk to finish reading the contract. I tried to glare at Ty through Lucien, and I was pretty sure he was doing the same back to me. After fifteen very long minutes, Cassie pushed the stack of papers aside and sighed.

"Faust's soul belongs to Satan as soon as he dies. He milked that for as long as possible, living a few centuries past what his normal lifespan should have been. But the moment he died, his soul became forfeit."

"See? I told you so."

That was the absolute wrong thing for Lucien to say. Cassie gave him a glance that should have made him spontaneously combust, then looked at Ty who wisely took a step backward.

"Yes, you did tell me so, but there is one small fact you're overlooking. Darling."

I shivered when Cassie called Lucien "darling." I noticed he did as well.

"Faust is not dead," she continued. "Therefore his soul does not currently belong to Satan."

"He died!" Ty shouted. "He died and we collected. His current state of aliveness doesn't matter because his soul was forfeit at his death."

"Unfortunately the contract was poorly worded." Cassie made a tic-tic noise and shook her head. "You might want to take that up with this particular crossroads demon, or someone in your legal department that puts together the boilerplate contracts. The wording does not specify his soul transfers to you *upon dying*, to continue in your possession after that act regardless of his current state. No, it says the soul belongs to Satan when *the living being is dead*. Mr. Faust *was* dead, and during that time his soul was legally yours. Now he is *not* dead, and his soul no longer belongs to you. According to this contract, his soul is Satan's *only* when he is dead."

"Oh for fuck's sake!" Lucien threw his hands up in the air, then eyed a few items on Cassie's desk as if he were considering throwing them. Thankfully he thought better of the impulse, otherwise I had no doubt he would have been spending several nights sleeping on the front lawn.

Cassie picked up the stack of papers, tapped them to even the edges, then handed them out to Ty. "I have no idea what the lifespan of a resurrected squirrel is. Either way, you'll just need to wait until he dies again. And I suggest this time you don't allow him to escape and resurrect himself if you intend to keep him in hell."

Ty turned an interesting shade of red, then snatched the papers from her hands. "Squirrels don't live very long. In fact, some squirrels have very short life spans."

"Oh no you don't." I pushed past Lucien to get into Ty's face. "You lay one finger on my squirrel, and you'll be the one with a very short life span. You and your hellhounds stay away from him, if you know what's good for you."

It was an empty threat fueled by anger and fear. I couldn't kill a demon. I didn't think anyone could kill a demon except maybe an angel or Satan or God. I couldn't kill him. I couldn't do anything to hurt him. And I honestly didn't want to. Just being this close to him was doing weird things to my breathing, my heartbeat, my shaky legs.

And from the expression in his face, he was battling the same very unwelcome emotions as I was.

"He can't stay in your house forever, Addy," Ty warned. "And the moment he leaves, he'll probably get flattened by a car, or attacked by a neighbor's dog. Maybe he'll eat poison, fall from a tree, or a giant eagle will swoop down and grab him from off your lawn."

I sucked in a breath. "Not if I can help it." Then I turned and stomped away, shouting back as I flung open the office door. "And don't call me Addy!"

Slamming a door never felt so good, nor did stomping my way down the stairs. Drake half flew, half hopped beside me, hissing supportive comments. I managed to hold on to my anger all the way out to my truck, feeling it give way as I started my vehicle and pulled out to the road. Halfway home, the anger had completely faded away leaving me shaky and emotionally bruised. Damn it, I liked this guy. The first guy I'd met in forever that I was wildly attracted to. The first guy who I'd actually had truly mind-blowing sex with—both physically and in my dreams. The first guy I felt I might actually love, who might actually be the one, and he was a complete asshole.

Why couldn't I find a nice demon like my sisters had? Why? I whimpered something out loud, felt a sympathetic brush of Drake's wing, and pulled over to the shoulder where I put my truck in park and put my head in my hands.

And then I cried.

CHAPTER 14

ADRIENNE

I really didn't want to go to this party, but I knew Babylon would drag me out by my hair if I tried to cancel on her. Besides, I needed to get out of the house and get my mind off of everything.

I'd taken Rhoid aside and told him about the meeting. He was elated that he'd been given a reprieve, but knew very well that Satan's minions were going to be waiting for him to come out of the house so they could arrange for his "accidental" death. That was a problem. I didn't exactly want to have the squirrel living inside my house for the rest of his life, and judging from his response, he didn't care to be effectively imprisoned here either. Maybe I could build a little warded squirrel addition onto my house and enclose part of the yard? Rhoid could stay out there with his little buddies eating peanuts and hopping from cleverly created obstacle to obstacle.

It didn't sound fun to me, but this was all the squirrel's choice. He could stay and be a self-imposed prisoner in my house. Or he could leave and take his chances. I had a feeling that, in spite of the terrors of hell, Rhoid was thinking about choosing option number two. But not tonight. Tonight he and his buddies were going to chill safely behind the wards of my house while I drowned my romantic sorrows in beer at a bonfire and corn maze.

Rhoid was settled in on my couch, but I hadn't expected his friends to disagree with the plan. It seems they were looking forward to all the goodies a corn maze had to offer, and they were upset that Drake would be coming with me while they weren't.

Finally I had to inform my vulture familiar that he couldn't come. It was that or risk a temper-fueled squirrel destruction of my house. To console Drake and the squirrels about being left behind, I made sure several bowls of food were out, and put the television on. They were arguing which channel to watch and fighting over the remote when Babylon picked me up. With my luck I'd come home to find the remote destroyed and the television stuck on endless infomercials.

I wasn't going to let it ruin my night. I could always unplug the television and pick up a ten-dollar universal remote tomorrow morning if I had to. Tonight wasn't going to be me worrying about my house or the animals, it was going to be about meeting new people, not thinking about a sexy demon who'd betrayed me, and trying to enjoy myself.

Locking the door and setting the ward, I handed Babylon two of the dog food bowls, and grabbed another in one hand and the pumpkin bars I'd made for the party in the other. "Here. Help me put these bowls out on the lawn, will you?"

"So you're feeding all the neighborhood strays, are you?" She shook her head and placed one of the bowls by the garage.

"Just these dogs that have been coming by." I'd checked my wards repeatedly throughout the day but none of the hellhounds, including Yeth, had been by. It hurt. Yes, I'd commanded their physical bodies, then taken control of their minds, but that didn't mean I wasn't attached to the big, hairy drooling boys. The thought that they'd gone back to hell when my spell wore off and never seemed to have given me another thought hurt.

And Yeth… I thought we'd become friends. I thought he'd side with me against Ty, or at least sneak out of hell to visit, to let me know that in spite of what had gone down, we were still good. I'd thought that if he didn't care one bit about me, he might care about the frozen bits of liver I had bought just for him.

I'd thought wrong. But still here I was, putting out food and hoping that maybe I could still be friends with these hellhounds. What an idiot. They were part of Ty's pack. They'd probably been with him by his side for thousands of years. There was no way a few days of eating kibble and scraps in my front yard could compete with a very long and hellish bond.

"Are you sure you should be feeding stray dogs, Addy?" Lonnie asked as she sat down one of the food bowls. "What if they have rabies? What if your neighbors shoot them? Or call the cops? We're not living in Accident anymore. You have to do things by human rules out here, not witch rules."

She had a point. I wasn't county Animal Control, but I did make my living dealing with animals. Given their somewhat alarming appearance, I was concerned that anyone else who saw them might shoot them on sight. Could a hellhound die? Be injured by bullets? Or poison? Be caught in an Animal Control cage? Maybe it was for the best that they stayed in hell. I couldn't exactly have a dozen hellhounds chilling on my front yard and not end up with angry neighbors and probably a big fine from the HOA.

But I missed them, and I missed Ty, so I left the bowls filled with food and headed to a party.

Lonnie chatted about her day at work as she drove. I gave her an abridged version of what had gone down in Cassie's office, careful not to mention Ty. She obviously realized that was a subject we were not going to discuss tonight, and instead told me about the people I'd meet at the party, including a guy she wanted to introduce me to.

Derrick. Six foot one. Dark hair. Dark eyes. The chiseled jaw of a superhero. Owned his own business. Single after a breakup a few months back. I nodded along as she sang Derrick's praises, trying not to think about a sexy demon who sprouted horns, breathed fire, and drove me to ecstasy with a forked tongue.

We pulled into the farm, past the house and barn and a line of trucks and cars, to park next to a stock trailer. The setting sun had turned the sky a swirling mix of orange and gray as we walked through the mown hayfield to the bonfire.

Lonnie introduced me to a few people on the way in, then we grabbed a beer and made the rounds. Within half an hour I was chatting away with a group of guys about termite control while Lonnie was off helping with the food. Termite control probably wasn't the most party-worthy topic, but Derrick had mentioned an issue that had cropped up on an inspection for a home he had an offer on, and suddenly we were all about baits, termiticides for barrier and soil treatment, and more organic methods.

He was cute—really cute. If I wasn't moping over a demon right now, I might have tried flirting a little.

"You're really a wildlife control person?" Ralph grinned at me. "Like those guys on TV who wrestle crocodiles and snakes? Not like the guys who just go around your house and spray poison?"

I shuddered. "There's no reason for that poison. Insects, rodents, birds, you name it—they can all be removed from a home without subjecting them, yourselves, your family, or your pets to harmful substances."

That was the line I gave when someone wanted me to throw down bait for mice. Clients were often skeptical, but I got results. Of course, I got them with magic, but no one this side of Accident's wards knew that.

"So for rodents you use those humane traps?" Derrick was looking skeptical. "When you let them go, don't they just head right back inside the house? And how does that work for termites?"

"I do use humane traps when I need to, and I make sure to relocate the animals as far away from homes as possible. As for insects, I have a method where they will move their activity to a suitable place. For termites, that's usually a rotted tree trunk that I put up for them."

Ralph snorted. "And when they're done with that, they go right back to the house and you get to collect another fee."

"No, they won't ever return to your house." I held up my hand. "Money back guarantee."

"How do you do that?" Derrick asked.

"Magic." I winked and they laughed. "It's a trade secret. If I let everyone know, all my competitors would be taking my clients away."

None of my competitors could do what I did, but Ralph and Derrick didn't need to know that.

"I'll see if the sellers will agree to hire you," Derrick vowed. "And if they don't, I'll have you come in after closing to make sure they actually got rid of the little buggers."

Great. It was always nice to pick up new work, but I'd come here to make friends, and I wasn't sure if getting rid of termites in Derrick's real estate properties was a path to friendship. Lonnie was right, though. He *was* a good-looking guy. Awesome smile. Nice. Cute butt.

And there was zero spark between us, darn it.

I left him and Ralph and weaved through the crowd, grabbing another beer from the cooler and trying to decide how to insert myself into a conversatsion at a party where everyone seemed to know everyone besides me.

"You're Lonnie's friend?" a woman asked. She had a long blonde ponytail and was wearing an incredibly tight tank top with jean shorts and bright purple sneakers.

"Her sister, Adrienne." I smiled at the woman. "You're…?"

"Rita. I know Lonnie from the gym."

I nodded, wondering if I should join the gym. "I just moved here from Accident. Lonnie's been nice enough to take me around and introduce me to some of her friends."

"Accident?" Rita wrinkled her pert nose. "That's the little town in the valley about twenty miles east, isn't it? I think we went there once a few years ago, but I can't really remember."

That would be because of the wards. Humans who came into Accident forgot about all they'd seen once they left. It kept our supernatural citizens safe from discovery. Trusted humans who'd decided to make their home with us had charms that kept their memories intact. If they ever moved, they were sworn to secrecy. Nobody wanted to get on the bad side of a town full of witches, shifters, fae, and vampires, so humans took those oaths seriously. Plus after living with us for years, or even decades, they were friends and wouldn't betray us.

But Rita and her buddies? They would have had a good time, perhaps a little freaked out by the "costumes" or other unusual sights, then gone home to have blurred memories of a good time—not *too* good a time, though.

"Yeah, it's where I grew up." Nostalgia hit me hard. "It was just too far to commute for my job, so I moved."

"What do you do?"

"Pest and wildlife control." I waited for the "ewww"

expression and was surprised to see Rita purse her lips in thought.

"That's cool. I love it when I meet women who have jobs that have usually been thought of as careers for men. Do you really wrestle snakes?"

I laughed. "They don't require wrestling. They're very nice, actually. Very cooperative. We have a pleasant chat, then I carry them out to my truck and relocate them to a place where someone isn't going to try to whack their head off with the sharp edge of a shovel."

"You're a better woman than I am." She tapped my beer with her own. "Are you staying for the zombie chase through the corn maze? It's right after we eat. I told Ralph that was a bad idea. People are going to be puking out in the cornfield, running around after eating like that."

"Zombie chase? Through a cornfield maze?" Wow, that sounded like fun.

Rita nodded. "It'll be pitch dark by then, so super fun and scary. About ten of us are designated as zombies, but you won't know who until you get out there. You'll get flags to stick in your waistband. Anyone who makes it to the end of the maze with their flag, gets a prize."

"And the zombies are wearing costumes?" I asked.

"Hell yeah. We've got a few masks and some old Halloween getups that our zombies are going to throw on to make it fun." She giggled. "I hope Derrick is one of the zombies. I wouldn't mind it if he tackled me and grabbed my…flag."

I laughed. "Maybe you should take charge and be the one pursuing a zombie instead."

"I might just do that." Her gaze drifted over to the man in question, then back to me. "You're not interested, are you? I don't want to step on your toes if you're working that."

I was so not working that. Aside from a possible business contact, that is.

"Nope. I'm getting out of a very brief relationship and am just looking for friends right now."

She clinked her beer bottle against mine again. "Then count me in. And to commemorate our new friendship, let me introduce you to the Jell-O shot table."

Rita and I did a few rounds of Jell-O shots, decided we were going to start taking Crossfit classes together starting a week from Monday, and made plans to meet for coffee Sunday morning. We were just selecting a third round of shots when someone whistled and announced that they were about to start the zombie run through the corn maze. Rita and I staggered over, met Lonnie at the table where two women were distributing flags, and helped each other tuck the scraps of fabric into our waistbands, all the while giggling about whether we should tie them to our underwear or not.

Sure. Why not? It wouldn't really be cheating, especially since we'd be running the risk of a massive wedgie.

We got in line, Rita in front of me and Lonnie behind me. Ralph came by and gave us a full beer for liquid courage, and we inched our way to the entrance of the corn maze. We each got a ten second head start. I was number six in line and by the time Rita took off, I was already hearing the screams and shrieks from the corn maze. I grinned, bouncing on my feet with excitement.

"No cell phone, right?" Derrick asked as I stepped up to the entrance of the maze.

"Nope." There was a full moon peeking from scattered clouds, and outside the corn maze the farm was lit up in shades of gray. It was dark enough to make everything more than five feet away a shapeless blur, but light enough that you wouldn't accidently run into the side of the barn. I expected it would be a bit darker in the corn maze, which would add to the spookiness of the game.

And once the moon went behind the clouds, we'd all be stumbling around in the dark.

"Go!"

On Derrick's command I took off running. The path split three ways fifty feet in. Going on instinct, I went left. That's when I discovered that I'd been horribly wrong about the amount of light in this corn maze.

It was dark. It was insanely dark.

The corn had been planted eighteen inches apart, but the dried leaves hindered the moonlight from reaching down through the rows. I turned right, then left, then right again, trying to ensure that my general direction would be straight through the maze. But was the exit on the opposite side from the entrance? Maybe it wasn't after all.

It wasn't only the location of the exit that was a mystery, it was my actual location as well. Surrounded by tall corn and unable to see more than a foot in front of me, I had no idea which direction I was headed. Paths curved, forked, made what seemed to be broad circles. I hadn't seen a soul from the moment I'd entered the maze, and their shouts and screams seemed oddly distant.

How big was this fucking cornfield? And where the hell was I? I shivered at the thought that I might be wandering around here all night. Hopefully Lonnie would sober up enough to realize I was missing and send a search party after me with flashlights.

Trying to sober up myself, I slowed down and took note of how many turns I was making. I looked up, but the moon was nowhere to be seen, and all this damned corn looked the same.

Shit. I was completely lost. Worse, people who'd come before me had trampled some of the corn and I could no longer tell which was the narrow path and which was just the space between rows. To my left the dried corn rustled and goosebumps broke out on my skin.

Like a rabbit, I froze. If I held still, maybe the zombie wouldn't know I was here and would move on to some other screaming partygoer. Then I'd run. And hopefully I'd make it out of this maze by sunup, with my flag still attached to my waistband.

What was I talking about? At this point I'd welcome a zombie. He could take the damned flag tied to my underwear as long as he showed me how to get out of this maze.

The corn parted and I saw him—a dark shadowy figure that seemed to have horns, his eyes glowing like hot coals in the dark. Fear—and lust—shivered down my back, and just like in my dream, I turned and ran a few steps, then stopped.

"Fuck you," I spun around to face the demon. "He's not here with me, and I've warded my house so tight that Satan himself couldn't get in."

Hopefully. I wasn't as good at wards as Bronwyn was, but a little bluffing never hurt anyone.

"I'm not here for Faust, I'm here for you," the demon growled as he took a step toward me.

I planted my hands on my hips. "Well, you definitely can't have me—not after the shit you pulled last night and at Cassie's office. Get lost, Ty. We're over. Get out of here and leave me alone."

I'll admit my voice shook a bit as I told the demon I was half—no, more than half—in love with to get lost. But it didn't matter how involved my hormones were in all this, I wasn't going to get all soppy and continue to have sex with someone who'd used me like he had.

"I'm not Ty." The demon took another step toward me.

Wait. Hopefully this actually *was* a demon, otherwise I'd just embarrassed the heck out of myself in front of one of the costumed guests at this party. No, I'd rather be embarrassed than have an actual demon after me. Ty I felt I could somewhat handle, but this guy…

Shit. The voice. The feel of him. The way his horns curved and his snout turned up. This wasn't Ty. And it wasn't some dude in a costume either.

I turned and ran. And this time I kept running. Just like I had in my dream, but this wasn't a dream and I wasn't completely powerless.

Reaching out with my awareness I found dozens of mice. I found snakes. I found a very pissed off fox, annoyed at us for disturbing his hunting ground like this.

Fox, which way is out? Show me the way out.

I heard his silent "yes," felt his presence as he left the den and moved through the rows of corn. I couldn't see shit, but I trusted that a fox wouldn't lead me astray. I left the path and ran, finally hearing the happy screams and shouts of the partygoers as well as the mock moans of the "zombies." What I didn't hear was the growl of the demon or the sound of him close behind me. Had it been my imagination? The beer, the dream, the darkness and the adrenaline of the game…had they all combined to make me see things that weren't here?

Either way, I was following this fox and getting the heck out of this maze.

I ran for what felt like hours, the corn stalks catching on my hair and clothes. A light glimmered off to my right and I hesitated, not sure whether to follow the fox's presence or head to the light. In a split second decision, I turned toward the light.

As I fought my way through the corn I heard someone coming toward me. Spinning around, I saw the demon once more. The light, I ran toward it, hoping that the demon wouldn't try to grab me once I was out among a group of humans. Common sense told me there was safety in numbers, but was there? Would a demon really give two shits about snatching me in front of witnesses? Would he care whether he hurt the humans or not? Could Babylon and I manage to fight him off before he did hurt someone?

Screw it. I'd rather face this guy out in the open than here in a corn maze. I took off, plowing through stalks in as straight of a line as I could toward the light. A shadow appeared in front of me, and before I could swerve or put on the breaks I slammed into him.

We went down. Flesh and blood. Arms went around me, and I looked up into his face in the dim moonlight.

Ty. My body reacted as if I had suddenly landed the starring role in a porno. I caught my breath and one of his hands drifted lower to grip my ass.

Then I got a grip on my hormones and remembered I was pissed at this demon. Although, there was another demon after me, and if I had to pick between the two, I'd pick Ty. At least I knew deep down in my heart that he wouldn't harm me. He might kill my squirrel, but he wouldn't harm *me*.

Still I scrambled to my feet, making sure I rubbed up against Ty a little on the way up. "There's a demon after me," I told him, figuring he'd do the chivalrous thing.

"Who?" he snarled, leaping to his feet.

"A dude with horns?" How the fuck was I supposed to know who he was? It's not like he had a nametag on or something.

"Abraxas," he spat out.

I'd been on the verge of running away, but that stopped me dead in my tracks. The horns didn't ID the demon. They all had horns. Ty knew who was following me. He knew this demon was after me.

Which made me even more pissed off at him. Damn it. He could have warned me when we were in Cassie's office. Although to be fair, we'd been too busy arguing for him to probably get a word in edgewise about there being a price on my head. Did Lucien know about this? Because Cassie was going to chop off his balls once I told her.

Something crashed through the corn. I didn't have time to see what it was or even run before Ty had shoved me out of the way and slammed into whatever it was. I landed hard, knocking the wind out of my lungs. I'd broken a few cornstalks in my fall and those suckers were sharp. That's how I knew the wet feeling on my shoulders and arms was blood. But all that seemed of minor importance compared to the epic battle going on not ten feet away from me.

Two demons fighting was like watching National Geographic alpine ram edition. They slammed into each other, horns locked, curls of sulfur-smelling smoke puffing from their nostrils and mouths.

"She's mine," Ty roared. Claws extended from his hands and he raked bloody furrows along the other demon's chest.

"If you're too weak to make her give up Faust, then I'll do it," the other demon snapped. I noticed that although he too had claws on his hands, he didn't seem to be causing quite as much damage as Ty was.

Wait, was I rooting for Ty? Yes, I was. Damn it. I was pissed off at the guy, but I still lov…liked him. Kinda.

The demon I kinda sorta liked head butted the other one, then punched him hard enough to send him into the corn. Ty wheeled around and grabbed me, pulling me up by my arm and dragging me down a path.

"No! There. The exit." I pointed toward the light only to have Ty haul me off in the opposite direction.

"That's not the exit, it's just a big spotlight at the edge of the field."

"Then where's the exit?" I snapped as I spun around, yanking away from Ty.

"I'm taking you there." Mumbling a curse, he grabbed me,

slung me over his shoulder and took off at a dead run. Demons could really haul ass, evidently. We were out of the corn maze in no time, with me breathless and dizzy, my face pressed up against Ty's back.

"Addy! You've still got your flag…oh."

Ty slid me off his shoulder and sat me on my feet, his arm around my shoulder to hold me steady. I blinked a few times at Babylon, not sure what to say.

"That's not Derrick," she accused, as if she'd discovered me cheating on the guy I'd just met an hour ago, and was most definitely *not* interested in dating.

"No. This is Ty." I patted the demon's shoulder.

"Ty?" Her eyes narrowed. "The one who used you to get to your squirrel? Who had sex with you as a pretense to get into your house and steal your squirrel? The one who doesn't care about anything but that damned squirrel?"

"That's not true." Ty glared at my sister. "None of it. Well, maybe at first it was true, but once your sister seduced me in her dream, I've been completely under her spell."

"I didn't seduce you or enchant you," I snapped back, irritated that we were having the same argument over and over again.

Babylon suddenly grinned. "How about you both agree that you seduced each other? That's one argument out of the way."

"Which leaves the squirrel." I took a step away from Ty. "If I sleep with you again, don't think that means I'm going to hand him over."

"As far as I'm concerned, the fate of Faust's soul rests in the hands of the lawyers, and they've said—wait…" He caught his breath and looked at me wide-eyed. "You're going to sleep with me again? Does that involve sex, or just sleeping, because I've learned that the language of the agreement needs to be absolutely clear."

"I'll sleep with you again if I feel like it." I sniffed. "And it might include sex if I feel like it."

He took a step toward me. "So…tonight…are you feeling like it."

I bit back a grin of my own. "Maybe."

"Awesome." Babylon clapped her hands together. "Now that Addy has a boyfriend—but only when she feels like it— let's all go over and see who else came through the maze with their flags still attached."

Maze. Shit.

"Wait!" I reached out and grabbed Lonnie's arm. "There was another demon in the corn maze who was trying to grab me and…I don't know, abduct me and hold me ransom for my squirrel or something."

"He'd have done worse than that." Ty's scowled.

"He might still be in there." I glanced back at the maze. Suddenly the screams and shrieks coming from the rustling corn took on a note of actual terror. A zombie ran from the exit, shouting "monster," and I instantly knew it wasn't an act.

The corn started to topple, and not one, but three demons crashed out of the maze. They were over seven feet tall, red skin stretched over muscles a professional weightlifter would envy, huge ebony horns curling up from their foreheads.

Ty planted his feet. "Stay back," he commanded.

I wasn't sure if he was including me in that edict, but it didn't matter because I'd never been a witch to avoid a fight —or obey orders. Once more I reached out my awareness, calling all the field mice, the fox, a raccoon who was raiding a nearby garbage can, and about a thousand beetles.

The beetles got there first, swarming up the legs of the demons, biting and pinching. The demons ignored the attack, grabbing at the humans. One picked up a picnic table and tossed it into the bonfire, scattering burning logs and embers all over the ground.

The whole place was going to catch on fire. I hesitated, unsure whether I should continue to concentrate on my animal attacks that seemed to be ineffectual, or should find a fire extinguisher.

The ground rumbled beneath my feet and I fell to my knees, suddenly afraid that more demons were going to erupt from the bowels of the earth. What emerged from the dirt wasn't demons, though, it was the dead.

Or undead, rather. Babylon stood with her head thrown back and arms outstretched. Her bright red hair whipped around her face in some wind none of the rest of us felt. Bones rose from the ground, connecting and assembling into skeletons of the animals they once were. I shivered, somewhat unnerved by my sister's very creepy power. Bone birds took to the air, bone rats joining my mice in attacking the demons' legs. My skin crawled as I saw actual zombies, far from shambling, join the fray. I briefly wondered how the owners felt about having their ancestors brought up from the family graveyard.

Ty was battling one of the demons. Fire rose from their skin, leaving trails of burning grass and corn stalks as they grappled and rolled. Their horns were locked, their bellows shaking the ground. Each swipe of their clawed hands left huge furrows that burned with flame rather than bled. Ty seemed to be getting the upper hand, but that still left two demons for Lonnie and me to manage with our magic.

"You take the one on the right and I'll focus on the demon to the left," she shouted to me. I watched as her zombies and skeletons swarmed the one demon. He tore them apart, but as soon as the parts hit the ground, they reassembled and renewed their attack.

Damn, my sister was scary.

Determined to be just as formidable, I pushed my awareness out as far as I could, bringing even more animals to the fight. The beetles completely covered the demon. Flame licked out from the wounds their bites caused, but none of the beetles seemed injured by the fire. The mice swarmed, biting and darting away before the fire could get them. Flocks of birds answered my renewed call—everything from barn swallows and mockingbirds to hawks and eagles. They swooped in, tearing into the demon with talons and beaks, swiftly evading his flailing, clawed hands. The demon stumbled around, blinded by the birds, overwhelmed by the other animals attacking him. With a roar he vanished and the beetles and mice fell to the ground.

I spun around, expecting to see the demon appear somewhere else and renew his attack. When I didn't see him, I sent my animals over to help Lonnie. No sooner had they begun to crawl up the demon's legs, than he vanished as well. I turned to Ty and saw him standing with empty arms, a perplexed expression on his face.

I ran to him and asked, "Where did they go?" reluctant to send my animal army away until I was sure the attackers weren't about to jump us from another angle.

Ty's eyes glowed like coals as he scanned the field and barnyard. "They're gone. They've returned to hell."

"Then we won!" I did a fist-pump, adrenaline still racing through my veins. I'd never battled demons before, and knowing that I'd helped defeat three of them gave me a heady feeling of power.

"We didn't win." He scowled. "They left."

I eyed him, confused. "Yeah. They left because we won."

He shook his head. "We were holding our own, but the fight was still balanced and could have gone either way. There was no reason for them to leave."

"Unless." My heart stuttered. "Unless they were here to

just distract us. Maybe that Abraxas wasn't trying to capture me after all."

"He *was*." Ty growled. "But Abraxas wasn't one of the three demons fighting us here in the open. He'd tried to grab you in the corn maze, and when that didn't work, he went with a plan B."

I stared at him in horror, having a good suspicion what that plan B was.

"Come on." Ty grabbed my hand and started to haul me toward the cars.

"Wait." I yanked my hand free, looked around, and saw that Babylon was helping the others put out the fires. "Lonnie! I have to go home. Ty's taking me."

"Be safe," she called out.

Rita was next to her, spraying a fire extinguisher. She paused and raised a hand to wave to me. "Best, most realistic zombie chase *ever*!" she called out. "I think you may have won. I'll send your prize home with Lonnie."

I waved back, then ran to keep up with Ty. It was so weird that the humans still thought this was all an elaborate production, with the pyrotechnics getting a little out of hand. But nothing about humans should surprise me.

But there was no time to wonder about humans or the fire or if Lonnie returned the zombies to their graves. I was pretty sure my house was under attack, and I didn't know if even my best wards would manage to hold off Abraxas.

CHAPTER 15

I drove as fast as the car could go, using my demon powers to get us around corners and across intersections without crashing. If only I could teleport Addy with me, but that would involve taking her on a brief detour through hell that wouldn't save us all that much time and would probably freak her out enough to smash whatever tentative relationship we'd managed to knit together.

Someday I'd show her my home, but not now.

I'd considered leaving her at the party and teleporting to face Abraxas myself, but I knew that too would damage what tonight had healed between us. Addy was the sort of witch who needed to fight by my side, and she wouldn't like being left behind to catch a ride with her sister. Plus I wasn't sure she wouldn't blame the whole thing on me if she didn't see me confronting Abraxas with her own eyes.

I had no doubt what he was doing. He'd intended to capture and torture her until she gave Faust up, but I'd made it quite clear in that corn maze that Addy was mine, and under my protection. I'd planned to finesse my way around Addy's wards, but Abraxas wouldn't care about that. If he had enough time, he'd possibly be able to smash his way through them and grab his prey.

Those three demons he'd sent after us might have given him enough time. Actually, I was pretty sure they had, and that Abraxas had called them off once he had Faust. It was why they'd scurried back to hell in the middle of the fight.

Abraxas would defy Lucien, confident that Satan himself would back him up if he delivered Faust's soul to hell. We were demons and the ends most definitely justified the means with us. Satan gave Lucien a lot of authority, but he still was the one in charge, and he wouldn't understand his son's need to keep his witch lover happy.

I understood, I thought as I glanced over at Addy. It was why I'd backed down and decided to honor her eldest sister's interpretation of the contract Faust had signed. It was why I'd followed her to that party, practically combusting with jealousy as I watched her talk to that attractive human man. It was humiliating to admit that I was basically stalking her like a lovesick fool, but I was glad I was there when Abraxas had tried to snatch her out of that cornfield.

Fire burned beneath my skin at the thought of what he would have done to her. I would have killed him. I would have ordered my hounds to rip him apart then accepted whatever punishment Satan dealt to me for killing one of his favorite demons. I wouldn't let any demon lay a hand on my Addy, not while I still had horns on my head.

I glanced over at her again, feeling that alarming sensation in my midsection, as if worms were crawling through my insides, turning what had been fire into a river of molten lava. Shit. No wonder Yeth was such a puppy dog when it came to Addy. I was the same.

And as embarrassing as it was, I didn't want to be any other way. Her touch, her glance, her smile, did things to me.

Painful, and yet pleasurable things. I liked it. I loved it. I loved her.

Which was why I was doing one-fifty through the city streets, racing toward her home, plotting the murder of one of Satan's favorites. Would Addy wait for me? I'd probably suffer for thousands of years for what I was about to do. Would she live long enough for me to return to her once Satan was done taking his displeasure out on my body? Could I find her soul if she died in the meantime? If she was in heaven, could I beg to just have a glimpse of her now and then?

The thought turned those worms under my skin to knives. I might never see her again, but I'd gladly pay the price to know she was happy.

As we screeched to a stop in front of her house, Addy was far from happy. She let out a cry that nearly ripped me in half, then flung open the car door and raced across her lawn.

"No!"

She scrambled through the wreckage of the front door. I heard her sobs, but took my time getting out of the car. There was no one for me to battle, no one for me to kill. As I feared, we were too late.

The house…the house could be fixed, although I sensed that by breaking through her wards and damaging her sanctuary, Abraxas had wounded my beloved almost as much as if he'd hurt her physically. I followed her inside, watched as she searched the house, a singed vulture limping beside her.

"He's not here. That asshole took him!" Addy turned to me, her hands in fists, her eyes full of fire. I saw three squirrels emerge from the rubble of her kitchen at her voice, tentatively making their way toward her.

I gathered her into my arms. "I know. I'm sorry, Addy. I'm so sorry."

Her tears were a mixture of sorrow and anger. After a few

seconds she pulled back, and looked up at me. "He killed Rhoid. He killed him so he could take his soul to hell and torture him. How can he do that, Ty? How?"

I knew how. "The contract says his soul belongs to hell once he's dead. We're demons, Addy. When faced with that sort of thing, our impulse is to immediately make Faust dead so we can collect what's due to us. He's avoided punishment for so long. It was bound to happen."

I knew as soon as I'd said it that I should have just kept my mouth shut. She pounded her fists on my chest, shrieking in fury. "That's wrong! He might have been clever enough to weasel out of his contract for hundreds of years, then to escape hell, but that's no reason to kill him. Your co-worker terminated his life before it had run its course. That's wrong!"

I held her tight, let her rage and punch until she just slumped against me and cried. It hurt—not her punches, but her sorrow. Faust was an absolute jerk, and I shouldn't care one bit about whether Abraxas killed him or not, but I did.

I cared because Faust had been my soul to deal with, not that fuck head Abraxas. And I cared because Addy grieved over the loss of that annoying squirrel who'd once been a clever wizard.

I didn't know what I could do. If I went to Lucien, I'd be a whiny demon ratting out a co-worker. If I went to Satan, he'd laugh at me and probably punish me for not being the one with enough balls to bring Faust back to hell.

There was only one thing I could do. So I kissed Addy on the forehead and left her in the rubble of her house to do it.

CHAPTER 16

ADRIENNE

Ty left and I immediately felt bereft at his absence. Rhoid was gone. Gone. Dead. I'd never see him again.

Ever since Cassie took up with Lucien, I'd had a different opinion of demons. Yes, they had their business, and I didn't always approve of their methods, but who was I to criticize how God and Satan managed the afterlife of reward and punishment? Plus Lucien was nice. He adored Cassie. He went out of his way to make sure his infernal career didn't interfere with their relationship. I knew he'd made huge sacrifices in both his reputation and in his business decisions to keep the peace with Cassie.

And then there had been Hadur, a warmonger who was so gentle and devoted to Bronwyn. And Nash, a reaper. Eshu, a sort-of demon, although I honestly thought he might be a demi-god. Then Xavier, a crossroads demon who bargained the sort of contracts that Rhoid had agreed to when he'd been Faust.

They were wonderful men, even though they were

demons who had jobs that involved the punishment of wayward souls. They ate dinner with us every Sunday. They *loved* my sisters. I'd just assumed all demons were like them.

Then Ty had shaken my faith. And this Abraxas had completely broken it.

He'd smashed though my wards. He'd broken into my house and trashed it. He'd stolen a being that was under my protection, killed him, and taken him to hell. Me. A witch. The sister of the very witch who was mated to the son of Satan.

I didn't feel safe. I didn't feel powerful. I wasn't sure how I was going to ever sit down to Sunday dinner with my sisters' demon mates and make small talk with them when one of their own had done this to me.

I knelt in my trashed kitchen and cried, Oak, Pine, and Maple snuggling against me in sympathy. Drake came and perched on my shoulder, running his sharp beak through my hair. I turned to him, feeling his soft feathers under my hands. He'd been hurt defending the house, defending Rhoid, but he'd healed since I'd gotten back.

I guessed familiars had powers of their own.

I tried, my witch. I tried to save the squirrel, but the demon's fire was too much for me.

"It's my fault, Drake," I told him. "I shouldn't have gone to that stupid party. I should never have left you all alone here. I just thought after what happened in Cassie's office, that Rhoid would be safe here in my house, behind my wards."

It's not your fault. Drake nuzzled me again. *It's that demon's fault.*

I wiped my eyes and gave each of the squirrels a reassuring pat. It might be Abraxas's fault, but there was nothing I could do about it. Rhoid was gone, and somehow I'd need to figure out how I was going to handle all of this going forward. Should I move farther away so I didn't have to face demons once every week at dinner? Should I just mourn Rhoid and continue on with my life?

Or should I get off my knees and fight to get my squirrel back, even if he was dead? For fuck's sake, my sister was mated to the son of Satan. My sisters' mates were five powerful denizens of hell. I needed to fight this. Even if Satan refused to intervene and I lost Rhoid forever, I'd never forgive myself if I didn't at least make an attempt to get him back.

The first step would be to go see Cassie. My house wasn't fit to spend the night in anyway, and Cassie did live in our family home, the one we'd all grown up in, that generations of Perkins witches had called their home since the founding of Accident. I texted Babylon to let her know what was going on, so she wouldn't freak if she drove by here and saw the condition of my house. Then I loaded three squirrels, a vulture, and a bag of clothes into my truck, and drove to Accident.

* * *

"This is bullshit." Cassie paced back and forth across the kitchen, sparks flying from her fingertips. I eyed her in a bit of alarm. Would I be worried about putting out random fires for the second time tonight? Because Cassie was just as likely to start setting things alight as demons evidently were.

"Tell me exactly what happened," Lucien said. His voice was calm and even, but he was also sending quick glances toward Cassie that showed he was equally as alarmed as I was.

"I was at a party, and while I was in the middle of the corn maze, a demon came out of nowhere and tried to grab me. I ran, but he tried to grab me again, and Ty fought him off. He said the demon was Abraxas."

Lucien's brows knitted together. "Abraxas."

Cassie stopped her pacing. "Not that asshole your father's been fawning over for the last few months?"

Lucien nodded. "He has taken quite a liking to Abraxas. It's problematic. He's not likely to support me if I lodge a complaint against the demon. He'll say Abraxas was justified in using whatever force was necessary to retrieve a soul that has eluded us for so long. In spite of what the contract says," he quickly added as he saw actual flames flicker in Cassie's palms.

"But he tried to abduct *me*," I stressed. "Then he distracted us with three demons who attacked us in full view of a group of humans, while he was smashing through my wards and destroying my house to get to Rhoid. I mean, Faust."

"Breaking and entering," Cassie snapped. "Attempted kidnapping. Assault. Did I mention breaking and entering? And all that's before we even get to him taking a squirrel that was under the protection of my sister."

"My father isn't going to give a damn about Addy protecting Faust in the form of a squirrel," Lucien argued. "And he probably won't give a damn about the rest either. Cassie, darling, please try to understand the situation. I'm the son of Satan, but I'm *not* my father and I don't have his authority."

"I think we need to let Ty deal with this," Babylon interjected. She'd arrived not long after I had, and was in the process of making a big pot of coffee for everyone.

"Ty?" Lucien laughed. "He's the master of the hellhounds, and I'll admit that he is a powerful demon, but he's no match for Abraxas, especially with my father backing the latter."

"He beat the crap out of him in the corn maze." I wasn't sure why I was defending Ty, but I found myself absolutely incensed that Lucien would think my demon was no match for Abraxas. He'd wipe the floor with that asshole. Wipe. The. Floor.

Lucien's eyebrows rose. "With his hellhounds?"

"No, he took Abraxas on without any of his hellhounds, and won." I felt rather smug about that. "I don't know why your father likes Abraxas so much, because in my opinion, he's a boot-licking weasel."

Lucien laughed. "I think so too, but my father does have his favorites. Thankfully they don't seem to remain his favorites for longer than a few years."

Cassie stopped and put her hand on Lucien's chest. "And no matter what, you're always his son."

The demon preened. "Well, yes. Although he doesn't always support me or agree with me. He does allow me a lot of latitude in the areas of hell that are under my control."

"Then use that influence," Cassie insisted. "*Do* something. You can't let this sort of thing go unpunished. If witches were to think that demons could attack them, invade their homes and take what belongs to them without any sort of repercussions, then all the trust we've built since you and I met would be destroyed."

There were few things in this world that demons were wary of, and witches were at the top of that list. We could summon them. We could entrap them and deprive them of their powers. But together, mated, a witch and a demon were nearly unstoppable. Lucien might be the son of Satan, but with Cassie by his side, his power could rival his father's.

And he knew that. He also knew how much Cassie's family meant to her.

"I'll see what I can do." Lucien sighed. "I'm not promising anything specific, but I'm going to assess the situation, see what things look like in hell, then come up with a few solutions we can consider."

It sounded like a bunch of corporate-speak to me, but I was exhausted both physically and emotionally, and right now I didn't have the strength to argue. So I nodded, thanked Lucien for his help, and went upstairs to sleep in my old bedroom, curled up in bed with three squirrels and a vulture.

CHAPTER 17

I left Addy's, went straight to hell, then cloaked myself in the form I assumed when I was presenting myself as Master of the Hounds. Gathering my pack together, I went straight to the top.

Satan was relaxing in a giant pool of hot lava, a drink in one hand and a copy of the Wall Street Journal in the other. The paper kept catching fire from its proximity to the lava. Each time the ruler of hell would curse, shake the paper, and blow the fire out. I wondered how many articles he'd not been able to finish because the continuation had burned away.

"Well, if it isn't Typhon, the demon who lost Faust's soul." Satan grinned at me once I'd been announced, and waved me over to the pool. The paper vanished, replaced by a lit cigar. "With all your hellhounds, I was a bit surprised to have Abraxas be the one to bring him in. Although I shouldn't have been surprised. That guy's got talent. Promise. He's going places."

"Abraxas didn't find Faust. I did. My hellhounds located him, and I was working to retrieve him." I shut my mouth, knowing better than to accuse Abraxas of swooping in and stealing Faust's soul from under my nose. Satan didn't take kindly to tattletales, and he didn't care who got the job done or how, as long as it gone done. If I delayed, and Abraxas got the upper hand, that would only raise the other demon higher in Satan's estimation.

Satan puffed on the cigar and nodded. "So I hear. My son told me you were closing in on our famous escapee. Some of the credit does go to you, although you *were* the one who lost him."

I gritted my teeth, detesting that I'd forever have that blot on my record.

Satan saw my expression and threw back his head with a laugh that shook the firmament and sloshed lava from the edge of the pool. "I can't completely blame you for that one. Faust is one tricky bastard, and he had help from demons I'd thought I could trust. The fact that he escaped is as much my fault as it is yours."

Satan must be in a rare happy mood if he was actually accepting the blame for anything. I played along, protesting that he shouldn't take any responsibility for that. Faust had been my responsibility, and if I'd trusted the wrong people, that was my fault as well.

He waved the hand holding the cigar. "That's all in the past now, Typhon. Faust is in our hands. Now I just need to think of the right place for him to go for his eternal punishment."

"And that, my Lord Satan, is why I am here." My hounds came forward to sit by my side, their eyes glowing, their fangs dripping a viscous liquid that sizzled when it hit the rocky floor. "No one in hell is as motivated as I am when it comes to Faust's punishment. It's personal for me. He escaped under my watch, and that's something I feel compelled to punish with my very own hands."

Satan's eyes lit with orange sparks, brighter and fierier than the flame at the end of his cigar. "I'm intrigued, Typhon, but Abraxas has asked to be the one to punish Faust. And after all, he *is* the one who brought the reprobate back to hell."

"And left a damned mess in his wake that I'm having to deal with," an angry voice boomed from behind me. I didn't have to turn to know that Lucien had joined us. He was the only one in hell who spoke to Satan in such a way, and the only one who could stride right in the devil's personal quarters without being announced.

Lucien stopped in front of his father. "There was a reason Typhon held back on grabbing Faust. Issues in the contract for Faust's soul had come to light and they needed to be clarified before we proceeded. Abraxas jumped the gun. I'm in the mood to hoist him up on the rack right beside Faust."

Satan's eyebrows shot up. "Such temper, Lucien. It suits you. But I also appreciate bold action that gets results and Abraxas has demonstrated such bold action."

"Yeah, at the expense of our reputation." Lucien's reply had his father pausing mid-sip of his drink. "The contract had loopholes. If it comes out that we can't be counted upon to abide by our own deals, to withhold action until the legalities are clarified, then our annual numbers will suffer. Humans will be reluctant to sell their souls if the deal they strike might not be upheld due to the whim of some demon who decides bold action is more important than keeping to our binding agreements."

Satan sucked in a breath, setting his drink to the side of the lava pool. "Did we wrongfully collect a soul? What did the contract bind us to do or not do?"

The leader of hell had reason to be concerned. Wrongfully collecting and/or detaining a soul against the contract both parties had signed had huge repercussions. There would be an audit. There would be an oversight committee. Angels would get involved on behalf of the soul. Lucien's grandfather himself might get involved. No one wanted that, least of all Satan who hadn't been on speaking terms with his father since he'd stormed out of heaven so long ago, taking half the family business along with its assets and employees.

"We are *very* lucky," Lucien shook his head, as if he couldn't believe how lucky the denizens of hell truly were in this matter. "Faust's soul is indeed destined for hell, but it is only ours when he is deceased. Thus when he escaped and was resurrected as a squirrel, he no longer belonged to hell and should have been free from pursuit until after his death."

Satan let out a relieved breath. "Well, no one needs to know that we were pursuing him. And as he's dead now, the point is moot. He's dead for the second time, and upon his death his soul reverts to hell. Now we just have to make sure the slippery bastard doesn't manage to get resurrected again."

"Normally I would agree, father, but Abraxas has put the whole thing in jeopardy. In his rush to claim Faust and the glory of capturing him, he has put us at grave risk of a complaint and an investigation."

Satan sat up taller, tossing his cigar into the pool of lava. "What the hell do you mean? He grabbed the squirrel, killed it, and collected the soul. That might have gone a bit over the line of the contract, but that little fact will stay in hell. Who'd complain? Faust? If the oversight committee listened to every whining soul who claimed they were innocent and shouldn't be here, they'd be buried in cases. And if any humans saw, then they'd just think some guy killed a squirrel. It happens all the time. No one is going to go running to heaven about a squirrel."

"Abraxas broke through a witch's wards, destroyed her house, and took an animal, a soul, that was currently under her protection," Lucien snapped. "That witch complains, we're going to be buried in internal affairs shit for centuries. They'll find the loophole in the contract. They'll audit every contract we've done for the last two millennia. They'll probably fast-track Faust up to heaven."

"No!" Satan's bellow shook the room once more. A two-inch crack appeared along the floor at my feet. "Faust cannot go to heaven! He's ours. He's escaped us once. I won't allow him to escape again."

Lucien shrugged. "This wouldn't have been a problem if Abraxas had just waited instead of trying to showboat the whole thing."

"But it was just an early collection," his father argued. "Faust's soul was ours. We just moved the timeline up a bit."

"Normally that would be a minor infraction," Lucien agreed. "But the contract both Faust and our representative signed clearly states his soul is only ours *after* his death. As his living soul was technically not ours, there could legally be no early collection. It's bad, Father. This is going to be a huge mess once it comes out—and unfortunately it's going to come out."

Satan ground his teeth. "I hate audits. I hate oversight committees. I don't want a bunch of angels pawing through *my* contracts, overturning *my* decisions regarding souls based on some legal technicality. What can we do? What if we get rid of the witch?"

The fire in my blood turned to ice. No one was going to harm Addy. No one.

I forced my inner turmoil aside and tried to appear as if I were interested only in protecting hell's interests. "Lord Satan, she has six witch sisters—one of which is mated to your son. Getting rid of the witch would cause even more problems."

Lucien nodded. "He's right. Six witches complaining that we screwed up a contract, illegally collected a soul, and then preemptively silenced a whistleblower…Grandfather might decide this half of the family business isn't being managed properly."

Smoke poured from Satan's ears. "I don't give a damn what he thinks. This is *my* business. It's not his any longer. It's mine. I might have agreed to a complaint procedure and joint investigative processes, but he'll get hell back when he pries it from my cold dead hands!"

I stepped forward, sensing this was my cue. "If I may, Lord Satan. I have a proposed solution to this mess—one that will keep it all hidden away like it should be. All we need to do is make sure the whistleblower witch is happy and satisfied with the solution and she'll agree not to lodge a complaint."

Satan pursed his lips in thought. "Will she be satisfied, though? And her sisters? I *would* like to be able to see my grandchildren someday."

"I believe she will accept the solution I'm about to propose. And in the end, we will get everything we are owed. We just need to be patient."

Unlike Abraxas, I thought.

Lucien and I waited, surrounded by my hellhounds, as Satan picked up his drink and drained the contents, throwing the empty glass into the pool of lava. I wondered what else was churning around melted in that pool? Books? Cell phones? A half-eaten sandwich?

"Tell me, Typhon," Satan finally said. "Tell me your solution to this damned mess."

I took a breath, knowing he wasn't going to like it. Hopefully he liked the alternative that Lucien had laid out for him even less.

"The witch will want a formal apology from Abraxas, and her house restored to its former condition." I held up a hand to let Satan know I wasn't done. "She'll want Faust resurrected and allowed to live out his normal squirrel lifetime without harassment from hell's minions."

"I can't do that!" Satan blustered. "I don't know who resurrected him as a squirrel the first time or how they did it. Demons can't do that. I can't do that."

I nodded. "I know. I'm going to propose something different to the witch that I'm sure she will find acceptable. She's quite fond of my hellhounds. If we offer to make Faust a hellhound, a member of hell as opposed to just a damned soul, I'm sure it will satisfy her."

Satan scowled. "But he needs to be punished. We may have screwed up his contract, but Faust still owes us an eternity of punishment."

"We won't get any of that if she lodges a complaint," I pointed out. "Hellhounds might be denizens of hell, but they have demanding responsibilities. And they are not immune from punishment. Any demon who screws up suffers the consequences, even a hellhound."

Lucien nodded. "Even me. Faust will have an eternity of difficult work. It's not quite what we had planned for him, but it's better than the very real chance that he might escape us forever and that we'll be buried in paperwork and committee meetings for thousands of years."

Satan shuddered. "True. Okay, let's propose the solution to the witch. Typhon, you make damned sure she happily takes the offer because I don't think I can budge any further on this matter. I'll release Faust's soul to you immediately for transformation, as a show of good faith. As soon as she agrees, I'll have Abraxas go to her house with a group of his staff to apologize and fix her house. Typhon, you'll oversee the repairs to make sure they are complete and to the witch's satisfaction. And afterward..." Satan's eyes glowed once more, "afterward I'll punish Abraxas for bringing all of this to our doorstep."

The leader of hell waved a hand, dismissing us. Lucien and I turned and walked out, my pack of hellhounds following us. I left Lucien behind, heading out of Satan's residence and upward, taking a slight detour along the way.

Abraxas was supervising the punishment of those souls who ran dog-fighting rings. Demons stood around the edge of a pit, cheering as the damned scrambled naked in the mud, fighting each other with bare hands and their dulled teeth. Abraxas turned to look at me, a cocky grin.

I punched that smile right off his face, taking out a few of the demon's teeth in the process. Then I picked him up and threw him into the pit with the damned. "If you ever touch my witch, if you even look at her, I'll kill you."

Abraxas screamed in fury, spitting blood and a few other teeth. "You're just jealous, Typhon. You're jealous that I'm the one who got Faust while you sat around with your thumb up your ass. I'm in Satan's favor. I'm in Satan's favor and you're not."

I walked away, knowing that very soon he'd realize that the favor he'd worked so hard to gain had been very short-lived.

Then I smiled and went to claim my newest hellhound.

CHAPTER 18

ADRIENNE

"Would you like another glass of wine?" Ty knelt before me, holding the bottle. I got the impression this was the groveling I'd been promised. If so, I liked it. And I knew I was going to like the makeup sex just as much.

"Yes, I would." I held out my glass and watched as he filled it. Maybe I should have him peel some grapes and feed them to me.

We were sitting on a blanket under a tree in my front lawn watching as a group of demons repaired my house. They'd already cleared away the smashed drywall, broken joists, and plywood and were just finishing up with the framing work. At this rate, I'd be back in tonight, although they'd probably have to come back tomorrow to paint and put down the new carpet.

Reaching into a bowl, I fed a few of the liver treats to Yeth, then offered one to the newest hellhound. After years of eating nuts and corn, Rhoid was taking to his new diet like a champ. Oak, Maple, and Pine had been alarmed the first time they saw him, but they'd quickly realized the giant canine monstrosity was their old friend. Now they were curled up on his back, snoozing away.

He couldn't stay—not that I minded that. Rhoid had work to do in hell, and he'd let me know that this job was far preferable than an eternity being whipped on a rack. In fact, it was his own request that had made me decide to drop the issue and let the whole thing go.

I hadn't quite forgiven Abraxas, even though his apology had seemed reasonably sincere. I had forgiven Ty.

Smiling at the demon sprawled across my feet, I reached out to touch his shoulder. He'd come to the party to apologize to me, to try to make things better and had ended up saving me from Abraxas. And then he'd risked everything to stand up to Satan himself and bargain for a better deal for Rhoid.

He might claim that Lucien had done most of the work, but I knew better. Ty was my hero with horns. Mmm. I loved a guy with horns. And I couldn't wait to bring him to Sunday family dinner and introduce him to everyone. My very own demon.

He rolled to look up at me, capturing my hand with his. "I'm ready for the makeup sex anytime you are, Addy."

Me too, except there was a crew of demons working on my house and we wouldn't have any privacy. I glanced over at my truck, but I wanted something with a bit more room.

Accident is only twenty miles away, Drake told me. *Hollisters Inn has rooms available.*

Now that was an idea. We could stay in Accident for the night while the demons continued working, then come home tomorrow to a freshly painted, newly carpeted home. I could show Ty the town I'd grown up in. We could eat at the Stagecoach Diner, maybe catch the band at Pistol Pete's, have champagne brought to our room...

A whole night of makeup sex.

I stood and tugged Ty to his feet. "I've got an idea. Let's ditch this place. Yeth and Rhoid can supervise the repairs while we go and have a romantic day. And a romantic evening. And a romantic breakfast."

Ty brought my hand to his lips and kissed it. "Darling, whatever you want. For the next twenty-four hours it's all groveling and makeup sex. I'm in your hands, my witch."

Silly demon. "Then let's go, because my hands definitely want to be on you."

We got into my truck, leaving two hellhounds, three squirrels, and a vulture in charge, and drove to Accident.

Finally I'd met the demon of my dreams.

Accidental Witches Series

Brimstone and Broomsticks

Warmongers and Wands

Death and Divination

Hell and Hexes

Minions and Magic

Fiends and Familiars

Devils and the Dead (2020)

White Lightning Series

Wooden Nickels

Bum's Rush

Clip Joint

Jake Walk

Trouble Boys

Packing Heat (2020)

The Templar Series

Dead Rising

Last Breath

Bare Bones

Famine's Feast

Royal Blood

Dark Crossroads

* * *

Northern Lights

Far From Center

Penance

* * *

Northern Wolves

Juneau to Kenai

Rogue

Winter Fae

Bad Seed

ABOUT THE AUTHOR

Debra lives in a little house in the woods of Maryland with her sons and two slobbery bloodhounds. On a good day, she jogs and horseback rides, hopefully managing to keep the horse between herself and the ground. Her only known super power is 'Identify Roadkill'.

For more information:
www.debradunbar.com
Debra Dunbar's Author page

ACKNOWLEDGMENTS

Thanks to my copyeditors Kimberly Cannon and Erin Zarro whose eagle eyes catch all the typos and keep my comma problem in line, and to Renee George for cover design.